UNCHARTED WATERS

Tides of Fortune V

STEVEN BECKER

UNCHARTED WATERS

Chapter 1

STEVEN BECKER

Leaving behind a fortune is never easy, and sure to be regretted. Although if the only other option is to remain alive, the decision is easier. Standing on the top spar of the rigging—my favorite place aboard our seventy-foot brigantine—my knees bent to the swell as the following wind pushed us toward the setting sun. As we sailed toward the horizon, it was this very quandary that occupied me.

We had "obtained" our current ship after the *Panther* was destroyed by a saboteur, leaving us no choice but to enter into a dubious deal with my mentor, Gasparilla's nemesis, Jean Lafitte. Just having been careened and refitted, the ship wasn't a sleek race horse, but neither was she the lumbering, leaky cow we had "inherited." Flying a full complement of sails under the watchful eye of Mason, our navigator, she moved easily through the seas. Our twenty cannon, purchased in Havana, provided our resident pirate Rhames with enough firepower to keep a grin on his face.

But it was Shayla who concerned me most. My love was fed up with our lifestyle. "Once a pirate, always a pirate" was the mantra of the Caribbean, including the U.S. Navy. Under President Jefferson, the fledgling service had grown into a respectable force, and with no wars to occupy it, the U.S. government had set its sights on obliterating piracy from the Caribbean.

The core of our crew—Rhames, Swift, Red, and myself—had started as pirates. My path was different than most. I had been abducted by José Gaspar, better known as Gasparilla, at an early age when he captured the ship our family had set sail to the Americas on. The old pirate had taken a liking to me, making me his cabin boy, and after several years I was adopted into his band. When the U.S. Navy lured his ship, the *Floridablanca*, out to sea and sunk her, Gasparilla rode the anchor chain to his death. I watched the entire affair from a nearby beach—along with a dozen men guarding ten chests of treasure.

Our small band of survivors had retreated into the dangerous and unknown interior of Florida, losing some treasure and men along the way, and gaining Lucy and Blue, while enroute to the Florida Keys. Our first true ship had been taken from pirates in the Snake River, where we found Mason, our navigator, chained in the hold. It had been my singular purpose since then to be anything *but* a pirate, which had turned out to be harder than it sounded.

Instead of plying the waters and robbing others, we had done quite nicely recovering gold, silver, and jewels from the deep. But being branded with the label of "pirate" meant we had no friendly ports to trade our newly found riches. That dilemma had forced our decision to head to the Pacific, where we hoped to start fresh.

It was our only path to legitimacy, and as we headed due west toward Mexico, I knew it was the right move. Our deal with Lafitte had cost us five-eighths of what we had recovered from the wreck of our own ship. This was the treasure that had just disappeared below the horizon, along with the three Spanish frigates that stood guard over it.

What Lafitte's crew didn't know was that we had part of Moses Henriques's treasure hidden in our holds. The little-known Jewish pirate, who had taken down the 1628 Spanish Plate Fleet, and I shared a common heritage. Centuries removed, I never knew him, though I had been trusted by another Sephardi with at least one of Henriques's secrets. Those riches now lay in our bilge, covered with a modest layer of stone.

With both funds and a seaworthy ship, we finally had what we needed to reach our goals. Our largest obstacle was the Caribbean, an innocuous-looking body of water that promised danger at every port and often in between.

Blue and Lucy, the transplanted African Pygmies we had found in central Florida, were adept fishermen, hunters, trackers, and healers. Because of their fishing skills we would never be hungry, and even now they were at the stern rail trolling feathers with bent metal hooks behind the ship. Every so often one of them would howl in delight as a tuna or dorado was hauled over the rail. The cook would pursue the flapping fish, ending its life with a slash of his dagger before gutting, filleting, and salting the catch.

It was a practiced and efficient operation that kept us in fish, but for a ship at sea, fresh water was always a concern, and not knowing what lay ahead, our limited supply was my top priority.

With regret, I left the rigging and climbed down the mast, and with legs acclimated to the swells, landed gently on deck. Moving back to the sheltered helm, I went to the binnacle, where Mason stood in his usual spot, studying an old chart and calling course corrections to the freedman at the wheel.

"Any regrets about leaving the treasure?" I asked, wanting to take measure of the crew.

"Only a fool would have tangled with three frigates. Even Rhames wanted no part of that fight."

It was a rare situation when Mason and Rhames agreed, and in this case, Rhames had called the retreat. Usually one to fight a snake bare fisted, it was a first for him as far as I could recall. But the decision to run would haunt us until we spotted another sail or land—neither auspicious signs for us.

"Panama?" Mason asked.

The isthmus had been our stated destination. From there we would have to decide if we would cross by land, or make our way down the coast of the southern continent and around the Horn. That decision could wait for now.

"We've got plenty of fish." We both laughed as Blue hauled another dorado over the rail. Larger than the schoolies, the cook pursued the electric blue fish as it slammed against the deck. Of all the species we had caught, the dorado fought equally as hard in the water as on deck.

"It's fresh water I'm concerned about," I said.

Mason waved his hand at the chart. "Not much choice for provisions."

"There're plenty of choices, just none that'll welcome us."

"The Pacific …" I started.

"I know, it'll all be different on the other side."

He was the skeptic aboard. Rhames, Red, and Swift, the remaining pirates, were the adventurers, not caring where we went. Shayla was pragmatic and knew our only chance was to find waters where we weren't known. The crew, now half of what it had once been, was rounded out by Haitian freedmen, rescued during our adventure there. We'd left one ship in Great Inagua after putting down a mutiny of sorts. I had offered three options to the contingent of freed slaves: stay ashore and work; take over our other ship, the *Cayman*, and try to make a living from the salt trade (of which Inagua had ample supply); or join my ship. Those who had signed on with me had blended into the crew and readily took to their training.

Studying the map, the first thing I noticed was the lack of navigational choices. Havana lay about a hundred miles due south. Landing on Cuba after being stalked by the Spanish frigates didn't sound like a good idea. Toward the west, three hundred miles away, was the eastern coast of the Yucatan— waters plied by Lafitte. Circumnavigating Cuba to the east was safer, but I wasn't sure we had enough fresh water for the six-hundred-mile crossing. Also, that route added a thousand miles to our journey to reach Panama. From our experience, with that much water between us and our goal, something bad was bound to happen.

"Friendly waters and a thousand miles, or make a run for Mexico and hope to slip past Lafitte and the Spanish?" Mason asked.

Rhames appeared. "They still want to hang us in Grand Cayman?"

"Not worth the risk there." But I saw his logic. By skirting the western coast of Cuba, we could make landfall in the Caymans, provision, and cross to Central America.

"Them out-islands there ain't big enough to hide a row boat."

He was referring to Little Cayman and Cayman Brac, both small atolls out of sight of the larger island, where I suspected we were still wanted men. Salvaging the *Wreck of the Ten Sail* had gained us a load of silver, but we had incurred the animosity of the governor there. "Six-hundred miles around Cuba, but only three hundred from there to the mainland. There's little chance of frigates in both them spits of land, and if there is …?" Mason said.

There was no need for Mason to finish his thought. Islands that small would have at most one frigate—a fight we could handle. If we were able to slip past Cuba, it might be our only fight before reaching Panama. Rhames was a gambling man, and if he liked the odds, I had to agree. Now, if I could sell it to Shayla, I might have a couple of days of peace.

Chapter 2

Without fail, whenever there was a stretch of peace aboard, an outside force would step in and remind us that we were still in the Caribbean. Leaving Amsterdam when I was twelve my family had sailed for a new life in America. I can still remember the excitement I felt standing on deck of the ship when we left port. It was an uneventful trip—until we reached the Caribbean. It seemed to always come back to that.

To a young boy, the thrill of the journey quickly faded as the vastness of the Atlantic spread out before us and the days started to blend together like the endless waves in front of the ship. Much to my parents' displeasure, it was during those weeks of relentless boredom that I learned to climb the rigging —there was little else to do.

That all changed when we neared Key West. At that time, the United States had little in the way of a Navy, leaving the Gulf of Mexico to Gasparilla and Lafitte. Gasparilla and his crew, several of whom were now my men, had taken our ship. I was separated from my parents, and never learned their fate, though I could only imagine it was bad. I still think of them, but time has long healed those wounds.

When the notorious pirate found out I could read, write, and keep a ledger, he recruited me as his cabin boy. Under his protection, I grew up amongst his crew and because of my literacy earned their respect. Gasparilla, being a former Spanish naval officer, was trained to document everything. He was purposefully lax in keeping a journal, as it could be used against him, but there was a thick, bound ledger in which the men's shares were entered. As the keeper of the great book of wealth, the mostly illiterate crew did their best to befriend me.

The route to New Orleans and the Mississippi River ran through our waters, and with the busy procession of unprotected merchant ships passing by we rarely left our corner of the Gulf. That changed with the growth of the Navy, forcing us into the Caribbean proper. Lacking the gold and silver mines of Mexico and South America, the spattering of islands cast on the aquamarine sea were used as pawns by the European powers, often changing flags as often as the winds shifted. Because of the unsettled political climate and the pirates roaming her waters, the Caribbean was anything but the tranquil body of water it appeared.

As is its manner, the Caribbean had lulled us to sleep, but the ship quickly came to full alert when the call from the lookout broke the quiet. Spotting a sail on the horizon was rarely a good sign, and as we approached the western tip of Cuba, we saw two. Word passed quickly and leaving no need to call the crew to their stations. With only two dozen aboard everyone knew their job. Rhames was in charge of the ship's defenses, though I had the key to the arms locker hanging from a leather thong around my neck. It had been part of our deal after the incident in Hispaniola, where he had attempted to make off with the treasure. It was a mutiny of sorts, although more to enrich himself than to displace me. He'd actually had a chance to kill Shayla and I, but allowed us to pass. In that instant I had looked into his eyes, saw his soul, and knew we were brothers.

After chasing Rhames, Red, and Swift down and taking back the ship, I'd saved their lives when the freedmen had realized their treachery and turned on the mutineers. It had always been my belief that there was something in his pirate makeup that made Rhames try mutiny, almost as if he didn't have a choice. He'd taken his best shot and after failing he seemed at peace with himself. We had an arrangement now, and holding the locker key myself was part of it.

Squinting into the setting sun, I could see the ships, but we were too far away to distinguish any detail. "I'm going to get a better look." I grabbed the spyglass and started for the mast, finding Shayla right behind me.

She took the spyglass from my hand and started to climb. "My eyes are better than yours."

This was no time for pride, and she was right. I followed her to the top spar, not failing to notice the sway of her hips as she climbed. Growing up among pirates, I had little experience with women before I met her. There was no doubt in either of our minds that we were made for each other, but our circumstances often placed friction on our relationship. She earned her keep as an accomplished diver and translator. Everyone aboard knew our holds wouldn't be full of treasure without her, but being the captain's woman was a constant source of irritation to her. We had planned to be wed on Cozumel, but as usual, something got in the way.

As I watched her scanning the waters with the glass, I promised myself to rectify that.

"They're flying Spanish colors."

I reached for the glass, more interested in the ships' attitude —how laden they were, and the cut of their sails—than the flag they flew. Most ships plying these waters had a full locker, as did we. Nationality was a guessing game when you had no home, and as I looked at our stern, I saw the stars and stripes of the U.S. flag laying out in the breeze. Well away from the Tortugas or Key West, thinking that no colors were better than flying the upstart American flag, I called down to the deck to have it removed.

A long time had passed since we'd spent any time in a port, and I was unaware of the current state of affairs between the European powers. Flying the Spanish colors would invite a meeting; anything else was a crapshoot. What we really needed was to evade the ships until dark.

"Keep an eye, love." I handed the glass back to Shayla.

"What are we going to do?"

"Run like hell until it gets dark, then sneak around the point."

"Always sneaking."

She said it without any attitude, but I knew what she meant. The sooner we could shed our pirate skin the better, and that would take a change in venue. The first step was to evade the ships now directly in our path. After the coast dropped behind our port side, Mason called for a turn to the south. It appeared the ships had mirrored us and were attempting to force our course into the *Golfo de Guanahacabibes*, a body of water treacherous enough that there was a large "X" over it on our chart.

In order to avoid that fate, we needed to work further west, but that had its own problems, as we would soon be entering the water patrolled by Lafitte. By now the captain had probably gotten word of the fate of his escort ships and our escape, making us a prime target if we were spotted.

"There's a shoal there," Mason said, pointing to a speckled area on the chart labeled *Banco de San Antonio*. "We run the channel between the reef and the mainland, maybe even the odds a bit." His thick finger traced the proposed course.

Rhames must have heard "odds" and was soon hovering

over us. "We make the first move and pick our line, we can load all the guns to one side, and lay twice the firepower on the bastards."

From the smile on his face, I expected he liked the odds. "How are we going to counterbalance the load?"

"Move the bloody treasure. I'll get my crew on the guns."

I hated the thought of uncovering the treasure that acted as ballast in our bilge, but there was little else to be done. Moving all our guns to one side would cause tons of displacement.

"We'll do what we can," Rhames said.

An hour later, the moon cursed us as it broke through the clouds, shining full and bright on the water. The details were lost, but the shape of the ships charging to intercept us was clear. Mason had set his course, choosing to run the western edge of the channel. This put us perilously close to the reef, but for our plan to work, we needed to force the pursuing ships to our port side.

With a noticeable list to port, we sailed toward the deadly shoal. Two men were on the starboard rail dropping leads and calling out soundings, but it mattered little. By the time their readings indicated we had encroached on the coral outcroppings, we would be among them, a position we had been in only too recently on the *Abrojos*. Running blind, we entered the channel and waited to see how the ships ahead would react.

I could imagine the grins on the opposing captains' faces as we brushed against the shoal, but as we had anticipated, they lined up to run our port side. Our fate was in Rhames's hands.

Chapter 3

STEVEN BECKER
UNCHARTED
Waters

The one thing we couldn't afford was to take a broadside from either ship. Pinned against the reef on our starboard side, we had little room to maneuver before the reef sliced through our bottom.

The freedman on the log-line called out six knots; fast for our ship, but looking at the frigates I could see the gap closing. Looking up at our sails, I called back to Mason. "We need more speed."

"We're flying everything we've got. 'Bout the only thing we've got going for us is the reef ain't in the lee."

Sailing a straight course, the frigates were faster, but as a lighter, smaller craft whatever extra speed our ship would give would allow us the maneuverability to evade the frigates and their deadly cannon.

"Whatever you can get. I'm going down to speak with Rhames." I didn't give him a chance to rebut. After a glance at the approaching ships, I estimated we had about ten minutes before they reached us. As I dropped down to the gun deck, the list was a bit less noticeable, but it still felt like one wrong step to port could capsize us. The men must have felt it as well, because they all favored the starboard side.

Rhames had doubled up the guns, two to a port. After checking the rigging that held them in place, I found him by a keg of powder.

"We're going to use whatever speed we have to throw off their aim, but it'll make it that much harder for you as well," I told him.

He smiled and chewed on his unlit cheroot—even our pirate wasn't crazy enough to smoke by the powder. "Aye, it will." He peered out the closest port to gauge how much time we had.

"No worries, Mr. Nick. We'll blow the bastards out of the water."

It was Blue who spoke. Despite the danger we faced, the Pygmy's imitation of Rhames put a smile on my face. He too had a cheroot in his mouth. Seeing him gave me an idea.

"Your magic that makes the smoke. Can we use it on our own ship without doing damage?" Blue was a master with his blowgun and I had seen the concoction of his throw up smoke before. We had used it on land as a diversion to throw our enemies into disarray, but fire aboard a ship meant death.

Rhames immediately saw what I was up to. "If they can't see us, we can't see them, either."

"But you'll know where they are before we throw up the smoke screen. They'll be taken by surprise." It was all I had. Changing our speed might throw off the aim of the first ship, but not the second.

"Aye. Give the bastards the slip, then. Me and the boys'll be ready."

With Blue behind me, gingerly leaning to starboard, we walked to the main deck. I nodded to Swift and Red. Along with Rhames, they made up our pirate contingent, and they acknowledged me with big grins. We weren't going to loot and plunder, but a battle still got their blood up.

"We're going to throw up a smoke screen," I told Mason.

"I'll get you a few knots, but there's not much wind."

"Whatever you can, on my signal." I left the helm to help Blue.

"You're sure this isn't going to blow us up?" I asked him.

"It'd be better to bring the skiff alongside and use it," Blue suggested.

That was a good idea. Calling to two of the freedmen, I gave the order to lower the skiff. They went to work while Blue and Lucy mixed up his magic powder. I tried to glance at the ingredients, but he was being secretive, and I left him to it.

There was nothing to do but wait, and I walked the deck, giving my best smile to the men. Looking up, I saw men crawling throughout the rigging and, as I expected, Shayla was up there as well. Many gunners aim for the mast hoping for a lucky shot that would take it down, crippling the boat without scuttling it. Even if the mast remained intact, the shot would surely damage the rigging. I wanted to call her down, but they were just as likely to aim for the waterline. There was no safe place aboard.

With less than a quarter of a mile of water separating us from the Spanish frigates, Blue loaded the skiff with several sacks and pushed it away from the ship. Crewmen, using lines tied to the bow and stern of the skiff, guided it to the port side. With a smile on his face, Blue nodded that he was ready.

With both sides braced for a broadside, there would be no premature volleys to test the range of the guns. When the first ship was a hundred yards away, I signaled Blue and banged on the deck to let Rhames know we were ready. Blue and Lucy each tossed a flaming torch onto the skiff, and seconds later we were engulfed in a cloud of black smoke. I hadn't thought about the wind, but it proved to be our ally. As well as concealing us, the cloud blew across the void, engulfing the other ship.

Not knowing what to expect, I heard the panic on their decks and orders being called out. Set free by the currents and with the small blaze aboard, the skiff would have to be abandoned.. As the first ship pulled even with us I heard Rhames call out the order to fire. Seconds later half our cannon loosed their projectiles. Across the void I could hear wood splinter and men scream, but before I could assess the damage, I heard their captain call the order to fire. We were passed the first ship now, and their volley flew into the gap between us.

The second ship was coming up fast and I called to Mason. The men in the rigging were ready and I heard the additional sails snap like a gunshot as they grabbed the wind. The ship jumped forward, picking up speed.

"Drop the painter," I called to the men holding the skiff alongside.

"Rhames, ready?"

The additional sails had given us a few knots. I could only hope the other captain didn't anticipate our increased speed as we came abreast of them. The skiff, no longer of use, fell behind us, and I could see the Spanish men's faces when I looked across at them.

"Mason, whatever you've got we'll be needin' it now!"

He called out an order and the ship lurched forward again. Just as it did, Rhames fired the remaining guns. The blast shook the ship, causing us to heel badly to port and the wind to spill from our sails. Fighting to stay upright and on deck, the freedmen and I were more concerned about ourselves than if the shots had struck their targets.

After a long pause the ship righted herself, and caught the wind again. Struggling against the uneven equilibrium of the deck, I fought my way to the port rail. Several of the freedmen were already there, and I could tell from the smiles on their faces that we were in the clear. The second Spanish ship was dead in the water a quarter mile off our stern and shrouded in black smoke. It had been unintentional, but the skiff had collided with it.

"All we've got," I called to Mason, who furrowed his brow, answering me with his expression that he already had every scrap of sailcloth we carried flying.

Our ship was a brigantine, designed to carry goods. She had been in a sorry state when we had taken her, but after making what repairs we could at sea, we had careened her on a beach in Cuba and spent two weeks arming and refurbishing. Our efforts had paid off, as she cut a nice line through the seas, leaving the two Spanish ships in her wake.

Chapter 4

STEVEN BECKER

UNCHARTED
Waters

With the threat mitigated we navigated through the center of the channel, avoiding the dangerous *Banco San Antonio*. Open water was ahead, but the channel had us sailing within easy sight of land. This close to shore I would have preferred to run dark until we were over the horizon, but with all our cannon still on the port side, we needed to balance the ship for both speed and in case we ran into another threat. Moving the thousand-pound guns was dangerous enough at anchor in broad daylight. At night, and at sea, the lanterns were essential to prevent injury to either crew or ship.

Rhames had the operation well in hand, and after checking with Mason I decided to inspect the ship. There had been no apparent damage, but I needed to ensure the ship had not suffered from the twenty projectiles shot our way. As usual, I started in the bilge. Finding it dry was a relief, and after moving a few of the stones, I saw the faint glint of gold in the light from the lantern. Relieved that our ship was seaworthy, at least below the waterline, and that our wealth remained intact, I climbed the ladder to the cargo hold.

The first thing I noticed was a thin layer of water coating

the deck of the near-empty hold and the chill of a breeze on my damp skin. Little air generally flowed through the hold, which, as it was designed to carry cargo, was built to be weatherproof. Holding the lantern ahead of me, I started forward. Inspecting each board as I went, I found nothing amiss with the forward bulkhead. Moving to the port side, where damage was most likely, I soon found a two foot in diameter hole blown through the ship. Avoiding the jagged splinters around the opening, I stuck the lantern, and then my head, out of the hole to inspect the damage.

The shot had hit a good three feet above the waterline, leaving us in no immediate danger, but it would need to be repaired. The seas were less than two feet now, but if they increased, we would take on water. Before heading up to assign a work party to make the repairs, I checked the starboard side, already suspecting I would find a similar exit hole.

Before I reached the bulkhead I saw the source of the water coating the deck of the hold. The shot had shattered our freshwater casks. After smashing through the inches-thick oak cladding of the hull, the projectile had lost momentum, and with it elevation, causing it to smash the dozen casks. Searching the rest of the hold I found the iron ball in the corner. The foot-around ball had put us in worse danger than had it holed us below the waterline.

After completing my inspection, I climbed back on deck. Mason stood by the wheel, instructing one of the freedmen to his course, and calling orders to trim the sails.

"We've got a problem," I said softly.

Mason slid closer to hear me. I detailed the damage and asked for a few men to make the repair. Though I was the captain, at sea Mason was in charge. He called three men over, and together we went below, where we spent the next few hours cutting boards, fixing them over the holes, and caulking the gaps. Without a real carpenter, the patch was rudimentary, but serviceable at least for now. It would have to be repaired properly, but our immediate concern was fresh water.

Back on deck, the ship felt balanced again, the gun deck secure and quiet. I could tell by the sound of the wind as it passed through the rigging that we were sailing well. I glanced back for the first time since we had left the two ships behind, and saw no sign of them. Trying to put myself in their captains' heads, and assuming they had sustained at least as much damage as we had, they would have abandoned the chase and headed to port.

Drinking water was our immediate concern. With hundreds of miles of sea between us and our next destination —be it the smaller Cayman Islands or the coast of Central America—the half-full cask of fresh water by the main mast was all we had.

I explained my thoughts to Mason, and we stood staring at the chart. Cuba was too dangerous, forcing us to broaden our search. The next-closest area was Mexico, several hundred miles away. If we were becalmed or ran into one of Lafitte's patrols we would be in dire straits. The Caymans were three hundred miles to our south, and the coast of Nicaragua was over four hundred miles to the southwest—both too far for a ship without water.

Isla de los Pinos lay barely fifty miles away. It was part of Cuba, but far from Havana and the busier ports. Although almost connected to the mainland, the shallow bay between the landmasses made transit by anything other than a canoe or skiff impossible. Because it was difficult to reach, the island had the reputation as a refuge for pirates and smugglers. We both agreed it was our best bet. Neither of us knew the dangerous waters surrounding it, so we agreed to heave to for the night and come up on the island at dawn.

Mason called out the command and in short order, the square sails were lowered and lashed to their spars. The gaff sails on the aft mast and jibs were backed, slowing the ship to a crawl, maintaining just enough momentum to allow for steerage. After seeing the tired faces of the crewmen as they climbed down from the rigging I was happy with the plan. There was a good chance we would run into another ship in the morning. I wanted an alert crew.

I relieved Mason as well. He would have stood at the helm all night, but there was no need. I knew sleep was far from taking me, and with Shayla beside me, we took the first watch.

"That's a bit of a chance, don't you think?" she asked, when I told her our plan.

As usual, even our best option was bad. "It's all we've got. The crew did well today."

"Hard to admit, but you were right about Rhames. Once he got that bug out of his butt that he could command, he's worked out well."

"Mason too. We've got a good crew."

I almost pressed her about the part where she said I was right, but I agreed with her appraisal, and left it at that. With nothing but open water ahead, I lashed the wheel and we both went forward. Sitting on the bowsprit, with our legs dangling in the air and catching the spray from the waves, I relaxed for the first time since we left the Tortugas.

We crept southeast through the night, knowing we would have to backtrack to the *Isla de los Pinos*. My plan was to approach from the east, using the sun rising behind us to blind any lookouts. They would see a ship coming, but not be able to identify her, or her flag. Before we were close enough for an observer to identify us, I planned on running.

Shayla and I kept watch through the night, and I woke the crew about an hour before dawn. I could see the tired look of men who had just fought for their lives, and knew they didn't have another fight in them. I silently made the decision that if we spotted a mast we would turn for the Caymans and take our chances at sea.

Once Mason took over command, I climbed the rigging. Even without the aid of the glass I could see a dark shadow between us and the fading stars on the horizon. It was a low line that I expected would soon become *Isla de los Piños*. I called down to Mason the direction the landmass lay, and climbed back down leaving Shayla with the glass.

"She's a good ten miles off." I stood next to Mason at the binnacle.

He traced a line on the chart with his finger. "This reef looks uninviting. Best if we come at her from the south. This cove in the Gulf of Batabano looks like our best bet."

He had picked a good, protected anchorage. The only problem was that anyone else seeking shelter, or laying low for nefarious reason, would chose the same spot.

"Good enough. Keep the sun at our back as long as you can."

"Aye." Mason turned away to give the new course to the freedman at the helm.

"Thinking we ought to prime the guns," Rhames said, coming up behind me.

"I'll run before we fight."

"That'd be wise, but better to be ready."

He stood looking at me for a long minute before it registered that he needed the key to the armory. Remembering what Shayla had said last night, I took the leather thong from around my neck and handed it to him. "It'll be in your care now. I expect you won't lose it."

A smile crossed his face as he took the key.

"Right, then," I said, not wanting to linger in the moment. "Sun'll be up in half an hour. Best get all hands ready."

Chapter 5

Illuminated by the rising sun, the eastern and southern coasts of the island looked deserted, but that wasn't where I expected to find trouble. Once we rounded the western point and got a clear look into the bay, three masts stood above the rolling landscape. From the configuration, it was a schooner, and faster than our brigantine.

Moving to the mast I called up to Shayla, "Is she flying colors?"

Spain's fleet, having fallen on hard times, was comprised of mostly brigs and frigates. There was a chance one of Lafitte's crews had captured this ship, but if it was his, I doubted he would anchor such a prize so close to his enemies. After seeking shelter in the rebel province of Campeche, the old pirate was *persona non grata* in these waters.

"Don't see a thing. A few men on deck is all," she called down.

"Guns?"

"I count ten ports and a half-dozen cannonades on deck."

Not only were we too slow to run, but we were also outgunned. Rhames sensed the same and joined me at the binnacle. With my focus on the masts ahead, I explained our predicament. "If you haven't heard, we took a single shot that destroyed the freshwater casks."

"Bastards. It's not just water we'll be needin' then. We need casks."

I hadn't considered that we had no vessels to hold any water, and though the island was covered with pine trees, we had no cooper. Making barrels ourselves was a fool's task. Our best bet appeared to be to try and purchase some. If not, we'd have to pirate them.

This was not a decision to be made lightly, or alone. I asked Rhames to gather the original crew members. They, along with a representative from the freedmen, would have a say. I'd learned the pirate version of democracy from Gasparilla, and seen its strengths and flaws. Having tried it in our own endeavors, I found it lacking. Ours was not a pirate enterprise, where the votes were often cast to displace the captain. After Rhames had tried his version of mutiny, I was firmly in charge, and seizing on his failure I had come up with our own version of the Articles of Agreement. Using the Dutch West India Company's format, I governed the ship by a "board of directors."

Rhames returned with the two other pirates, Swift and Red, along with Shayla, Lucy, Blue, and the freedman. The group, including Mason and I, would decide our fate.

"Right, then," I said, calling the group gathered around the binnacle to order. "I've had a look and we've taken little damage. One shot to the hold. It's above the waterline, and a temporary repair has been fashioned ... "

"What about the barrels?" Red piped in.

"I was just about to finish my report," I said, firmly. "The water barrels are in ruins. We've got only the half-barrel left on deck." All eyes instinctively turned to the sky, the logical source for fresh water at sea. It was a perfect powder blue with not a cloud in sight.

"Right, then. There's a ship anchored in the bay. We'll come about and cut off its exit, then pay them a visit. See if we can buy some barrels."

"Aye, if not we can liberate them," Rhames said, with a devilish look on his face.

I felt Shayla press against me, and reached down for her hand. "We've got enough gold in our hold to buy the ship."

I hoped that settled the matter, but a glance at Rhames, who, with his hand shielding his brow, studied the anchored ship. I knew he was apprising it from a military perspective and left him to it. Taking the ship was not our plan, but learning what you can about a potential enemy was never a bad thing. Moving away, I entered the companionway, and grabbing a lantern from a hook on the wall, lit it, and started to climb down to the bilge.

After extracting a handful of gold coins, more than enough for a few dozen barrels, I returned to deck. Mason had positioned the ship off the point with the starboard rail facing land. From there we controlled the deepwater exit from the bay. The schooner at anchor would be faster, but the shallows would limit her ability to maneuver.

"Lower the skiff," I ordered, and waited while the men manned the davits, which swung our remaining longboat over the side and lowered it in the water.

"Best be careful with her," Mason said.

After losing the first of our two skiffs in the battle earlier, I would need to make sure this skiff returned. Looking at Shayla, I nodded. We dropped over the side and climbed down the rope ladder to the waiting skiff. Not usually one to stand on ceremony, I did know when a show of force was warranted, and with two freedmen at the oars, and Swift and Red well-armed, I felt confident that we would return.

As we approached the sloop, I was immediately envious of her lines. The long waterline, narrow beam, and a sail plan that allowed efficiency despite the direction of the wind made for a fast ship. And I couldn't help but think how perfect she would be for a trip around the Horn to the Pacific. Looking around at my crew, I could see they had made the same appraisal. Putting the thought from my mind, I sat tall on the bench and prepared to find out who we would have the pleasure of meeting.

I silently noted my observations as we pulled alongside. Judging from the clean look of her hull, the ship was new enough to never have been careened. A rope ladder dropped over the side just as we touched the schooner and I heard a voice hail down to us.

"If you've come in good faith, you're welcome aboard," he said in English.

I looked over at Shayla, who had accompanied us in the event an interpreter was needed. I would have asked her to join the group, but that hadn't been necessary. I liked the fact that she was strong of both body and mind. With a fiery look in her eyes and pursed lips I knew she was coming aboard with us.

"Right, then." Leaving the freedmen with the skiff, I sent Red and Swift up the ladder with Shayla and I following behind.

The captain had a familiar look, but his coiffed hair hid his eyes. "Captain James Harp," he introduced himself with a nod. When he looked up, I flinched on seeing his blood-red eyes.

"Nick Van Doren, this is Shayla, Red, and Swift." I left the titles out, letting him guess if I was really the captain. It was common practice to have a seaman stand-in just in case subterfuge was on the menu.

"Refreshments are in order. Then we can discuss what we can do for each other," he said. Something about his voice grated on my nerves. Keeping our goal in mind, my wariness increased as he led the way to the stern deck, where a table and chairs were set.

"Get a measure of their weapons and men," I whispered to Red and Swift. With a fair amount of trepidation, Shayla and I followed Captain Harp to the table. It appeared to be a friendly greeting, but at sea, especially in the Caribbean where there was no one power that ruled, things were rarely as they appeared.

If he were plotting our demise, Harp certainly fed us well first. We were served something that at first I thought might be roasted pork, along with some root vegetables. Fresh meat was always welcome after bouncing around at sea for a month, and thought the taste was slightly off, I ate my share. It had been on Cozumel that we last had a proper meal. Along with the food was a better-than-average wine, followed by a good port. As our host had intended, by the time I pushed back my chair I was relaxed and in a "receptive" mood.

"So, what brings you to the *Isla de los Piños*?" Harp asked.

I placed my napkin on the table. "Fresh water and provisions," I said.

"As you can tell by our fare, you have made a good enough choice."

Something again struck me as odd and I wondered why his ship was anchored in this dangerous and shallow bay. His was too large and expensive a ship to be out of action for any length of time. Aside from the dangerous waters she was anchored in, there would be no income for the owners, crew, or captain if the ship was not working. There was always an attitude on a ship and I had been aboard enough that I knew when the crew was disciplined. The deck of this schooner was in disarray and she had a wretched air about her. In many ways it resembled a gypsy camp—or a pirate ship.

"Right, then. It's some casks we're after. Our Havana-bought supply has proven inferior."

That brought a smile to his face. Enjoying a joke at the expense of the Spanish was fair game here, but it brought a question to my lips. If he wasn't a friend of the Spaniards, who was he?

"What business are you about, then?"

I hesitated, knowing the answer was often misunderstood. "We are salvors making our way to Panama and across to the Pacific." I had come up with the term to describe us. Sometimes it was taken at face value, and other times it brought unwanted questions.

"Really, so you recover what others have lost?"

"Yes. We've become proficient at diving as well." I padded our resume, hoping to lend our ventures some legitimacy.

The smile that appeared on his face was different from the one he used when looking at Shayla. "It appears that we have need of each other, young Captain Van Doren."

I felt men gather behind me. Whenever someone used "young" to prefix my name it usually meant they thought they had out-maneuvered me. In this case, a length of rope was slung around me and I felt the abrasive fiber cut into my chest and arms as I was secured to the back of the chair. A glance at Shayla, Red, and Swift revealed they had met the same fate.

Chapter 6

While decisions were made regarding Shayla, the two pirates, and myself, I studied the ship and crew, doing my best to absorb every detail I could. Something or someone would be the key to our freedom.

I had been too interested in the ship itself earlier and failed to notice the ragtag British uniforms the men wore. No captain of the line would have allowed their appearance. Then there was Harp himself. His blotchy skin and red eyes led me to believe that he was ill, and now after being taken prisoner, I wondered what was amiss.

We were moved underneath a shade awning stretched over the boom and settled to the deck. I continued to study the men and ship as we waited, which confirmed my opinion that something was seriously wrong here. A large iron pot cooking the meat sat nearby, the area littered with bones and blood. The two men stirring the pot smiled at us, almost as if they shared a secret.

A few minutes later, I heard Captain Harp's voice from the companionway. Another man, who I didn't recognize, recited back the words the captain had just spoken to him, in a hushed tone. He stumbled over them several times, either from lack of familiarity or a suspect memory. I didn't expect he was the shiniest piece of brightwork aboard.

The one-sided conversation concluded and the man soon appeared dressed in the captain's finery. He would represent himself to my crew as the master of the ship, or at least try to. It was a common enough ploy, one that we had used several times, to allow the captain to remain anonymous. Harp gave him one last piece of advice and sent him down the rope ladder, where I expected our two freedmen would be tasked with rowing him over to our ship and back.

Mason and Rhames had settled into an uneasy alliance, which I hoped would last long enough to hear out Harp's demands, and act on them. Though they were both intelligent and rational, their experiences and expectations were entirely different. Rhames expected everything to be a fight. Mason was the opposite; he always sought a peaceful solution. Together the mix was often volatile.

"Captain, if I may ... "I called out after the captain's doppelganger had dropped below the rail.

Harp turned back to me. "I'd address you likewise if I knew you were actually the captain."

"I can assure you—" I stopped when I saw the skeptical look in his eye. Changing tacks, I offered a different perspective. "If I'm not, I don't expect we'd be much of a bargaining chip." I was younger-looking than my years, and with my average physique I would blend in to a crowd more than a captain should.

He rubbed his chin through the stubble he had grown to hide the blotchy rash.

"I'm also the owner of the ship. If you have terms it might behoove you to speak to me directly."

"I'll attest for what he's said," Shayla offered.

Red and Swift nodded their heads.

"All the better, then. You'll be my guarantee of safe passage."

He had countered my opening move of blocking his exit from the anchorage by taking hostages. I was faced with a formidable and possibly demented foe. "We'll gladly sail to your next port of call if you deliver to my ship the dozen water barrels we need." I reached into my pocket.

The minute he saw the glint of gold his attitude changed. "Well, young Captain. Where might you have come across a pocketful of gold?"

I knew right then it had been a mistake to bring gold instead of silver. When your ballast was loaded with riches it distorted your senses. A captain of an older brigantine would have a scant few silver coins. In an effort to impress, I had over-played my hand.

"As I've already explained, we've done some salvage work."

He removed his hat and rubbed his hand over his slick, bald head. "Maybe I was a tad hasty." Harp called to the crewman tasked with overseeing us and ordered him to free Shayla's and my bonds.

With the ropes removed, we stood. Red and Swift remained secured, tied back to back. I gave them a reassuring look and followed the captain to the quarterdeck. He offered wine, which, though I didn't want it, knew it was bad form to refuse. While I nodded in an unspoken toast and took a sip, Shayla took her glass and drank greedily. Harp did the same and motioned us to sit.

"Salvage, eh? I'm sure you have a few stories."

I thought before responding, not wanting to squander our newfound value. "The *Wreck of the Ten Sail*, in the Caymans, was one. Lately we've been playing cat and mouse with Lafitte and the Spanish." I said the former to give us some credibility and the latter to see if we had anything in common. Enemies sharing the same plight often became allies.

"Lafitte is surely a scoundrel, but his ships are slow and no match for this girl," he said proudly.

"And the Spanish?" He sipped his wine, but I could tell he was deciding how much to tell me about the conditions that led him to be anchored in a shallow bay and so easily penned in by a slower ship. Had it not been for our desperate need for fresh water, we could have taken him.

"No friends of ours, either. I'd have guessed that were you on good terms, we might not have found you here."

He sipped again. "And it appears that finding us might be to your good fortune."

"Before we go any further, I'd appreciate a barrel of water sent over to my ship."

"As soon as my skiff returns, Captain."

At least he had acknowledged me. "Alright, then. So, the Spanish?"

He poured another round of wine. My cup took little, but Shayla's was empty. Though not usually a heavy drinker, she and her father, Phillip, had been proprietors of a bar in Grand Cayman. She knew her way around alcohol, and I wondered about the reason for her need to imbibe. Seeing my distraction, Harp finished pouring and sat.

With a sigh he started. "The devil with them. Minding our own business we were, beating into the wind and making our way around this blasted island when two of their frigates started to chase us."

"Where about did this happen?" I asked.

"Just past the *Banco de San Antonio*."

These sounded like the same two ships that we had just escaped. It appeared they had lost the faster schooner and decided on taking us as a prize so they wouldn't return to port empty-handed.

"We outran them, but lost a ship to the reef," Harp said.

It occurred to me that if there was something of value

31

aboard the sunken ship we could be of service. "We've had some experience salvaging wrecks."

We were interrupted by the return of the skiff. Once the sailors and "captain" were back aboard, they came to the table and looked at me.

"Appears you've had the captain the entire time," the man said.

"Well, of course," Harp responded. "We'll talk later about what you saw aboard."

The man, with a look of confusion on his face, walked away shaking his head from side to side.

"It appears your story is confirmed, then." Harp raised his glass. "So, tell me of your salvage techniques."

I had no reason to hide anything, as there was quite a bit more to salvage than possession of the equipment required to reclaim what the sea had taken. Our hard-earned experience was invaluable. Leaning forward in my chair, I looked over at Shayla, whose cheeks had turned red from the wine. I'd seen her like this one other time and knew I'd have to get her into a bunk sooner rather than later.

Detailing some of our methods, much like a salesman pitching his wares, I gave a brief description of how we had learned to equip the dive bell and our success with it. He seemed fascinated, and I got the feeling that our skills might become a sought-after commodity. Continuing, I belabored the points of expertise required to keep the men alive underwater, and again as they surfaced from their dives. What I didn't mention was that the diving bell now sat in thirty feet of water in an area in the Dry Tortugas I had named *The Tongue*, a place I had no intention of returning to.

"Aye, young Captain. I get your point. If we would employ your services, what might we expect to pay?"

I had never been offered payment for our work; it had always been on speculation. Thinking back to how my father would have handled the opportunity, I started to question the captain, evaluating whether it would be worth a fee or a share.

"I'll have to confer with the crew about the work, but a deposit of the water casks would surely help."

"Then you won't mind if I keep your men here as surety." He smiled.

A half-hour later, with the freeboard of the skiff just inches from the water, we brought the half-dozen casks back to the ship. Mason and Rhames were waiting on the rail and supervised the offloading and storage. When all was complete and Harp's skiff sent back, I gathered the crew around the mast.

Chapter 7

"Cannibals," Shayla spat, and ran over to the rail. Wiping her mouth, she returned a minute later.

I had seen the signs but chose to ignore them. Feeling my stomach roil, I thought about Harp.

"The captain appears to be in the late stages of syphilis," I said. The men were all too familiar with the disease. Knowing Swift and Red were prisoners aboard the mad-man's ship, sullen looks fell over the crew assembled by the mast—with the exception of Rhames. That old pirate's face had revenge etched into it. I waited until they settled down. They might not all have a say in what was decided, but I wanted them to hear it from me, not secondhand.

"Bastard's got us over a barrel and the son of a bitch'll have my boys over the cooking pot if we don't do something." Rhames said.

This started a new round of discussion and speculation. Again, I waited for the men to settle down. Rhames was ready to load up and take the ship, but I knew, despite the disorder and lack of discipline aboard the schooner, she still outmanned and outgunned us.

"Red and Swift are safe for the time being. Harp needs us. He's given us some casks and a bit of water, but not enough to safely see us anywhere without a rainstorm to replenish it." I told them about the ship Harp claimed the Spanish had sunk by the reef. "I say we see what we can salvage and get our men back."

"If it don't work out it's going to be bad for me boys," Rhames reminded everyone.

With a determined look on her face, Shayla turned to look at the schooner. "We can't allow that to happen."

It wasn't often the two of them agreed. I exchanged looks with both of them. "As long as we work with him, they'll be safe enough."

Most of the freedmen were nodding in agreement. Without Red and Swift, Rhames was just one vote. It was Shayla I was concerned with. Numerically, her vote counted the same as everyone else; however, seeing the two of us split in our opinion was not good for morale. Faced with choosing to have a discussion in front of the men or in private, I chose the latter, knowing her quick mind and wit were liable to embarrass me in front of the crew. Most times she was good at reading situations, but with her mind made up about something, as it appeared to be now, she would fight to the death. If there was to be blood, I'd rather it flow in the privacy of our cabin than on the deck.

I adjourned the crew, promising a vote before we weighed anchor. Shayla continued to stare at the schooner, assuring me that I had taken the coward's way. With a red face, she marched toward the companionway and disappeared belowdecks. There was nothing I could do to mitigate my embarrassing position with the crew, so I followed. The best I could hope was to sway the inevitable talk of who actually ran the ship by convincing her that my option was best.

"We've dealt with men that can't be trusted before," I started.

She turned to face me. "And how has that worked out for us? Just because we have the ability to help the demented fool doesn't mean we should."

I rethought my position, trying to ensure I was doing the best for my ship and crew and not indulging myself in a salvage effort to impress myself or Harp. It wasn't an easy decision, and as I thought about it I considered the larger circumstance. We were still without a country, at-large in the hornet's nest of the Caribbean, and identifiable to most as pirates.

"Six casks at about thirty gallons each is enough water for less than a week, and that's if they don't sour or spill," I told her. I hoped a little math might show her the reality of our situation without contradicting her. "Assuming the trades hold, we can cover just around a hundred miles per day. And there's no guarantee the anchorage we find will be safe or have water available."

She was quiet for a few minutes. "Supposing you're right, but Harp breathes deceit. It hangs on him like cheap perfume."

There was no denying her that. "If I told you my goal was to take his ship, what would you say?" I hadn't wanted to say it out loud—or now—but, as Harp had turned out to be an enemy, we would have good reason to take his ship. And that ship was capable of rounding the Horn.

She nodded.

"So, you'll go along?" I asked, wanting to confirm.

"Yes, but between you and me, we're getting those two pirates back and taking the bloody schooner out from under him."

I tried to keep the smile from my face as I went above to gather the crew again. Shayla followed a few minutes later. I was glad to have her beside me rather than have to relay her feelings second-hand. Her voice would be stronger if she was present.

"We'll take the dozen casks and a half-share of what's recovered. That'll be the deal. First sight of a Spanish flag and we're off to the Caymans."

"Aye," Rhames called out. "What about me boys?"

"I'll demand they be released before we get in the water."

That seemed to satisfy him for the time being. With Rhames and Shayla in agreement we were decided. I sent a messenger to Harp's ship with our terms, and should he accept them we would proceed to the site at first light.

Several hours of daylight remained, so I had the men haul the diving gear on deck. We hung a block and tackle from the boom, which would allow us to retrieve what we found. The hoses we had fashioned in Cozumel were laid out in the shade of a rigged awning so the sun would not dry out the lard they were coated with, then we inspected them as well. Assembling the divers, we set a schedule. Everything was ready, and under the light of the moon we rolled up the hoses and stowed the gear.

When the men finished, I climbed the mast and relieved the freedman on watch. It was my habit to take a watch, as much to relieve our short-handed crew of the duty as to escape the confines of the ship. After a quick glance at the approaches, I turned my attention to the schooner anchored less than a quarter mile away.

She was everything we could ask for in a boat, and now we had the justification to take her. Lanterns illuminated the deck of the ship, usually a sign that the captain was either brazen or stupid, but in this case, it happened that he was demented. The island concealed his ship from the sea, but on a clear night such as this his lights could easily be seen from the mainland. If he wanted to avoid trouble from the Spanish, this was not how to go about it. Swedish colors flew from her mast, but I knew that to be a ruse. Many American merchants, unwilling to suspend their trade during the recent war, had brought in enough Swedish investors to change their ship's registries and avoid the blockades.

Because of his condition, Harp's motives were hard to identify. On the surface, despite the colors she flew, she and her crew were clearly British. As I stared down at the schooner, his game became apparent. The personal reasons for his betrayal to the Union Jack were irrelevant. He had clearly taken the ship. It was well known that transporting sugar from Havana to the northern Atlantic was extremely profitable right now, and I surmised the schooner had been designated an escort vessel, removing the crew and captain from any profit. Harp had turned on the crown. Rather than escort the ships north, he *"escorted"* them to his own dealers, who bought the sugar from *him*.

Though I had been raised by pirates, Gasparilla, originally a Spanish officer, had made sure my education was of the formal variety, and excluded pirate lore. His crew had a different opinion of what an education should be, and told me stories of the great pirates, many from first-hand experience. Harp wasn't the first naval officer to turn pirate. Gasparilla had done the same, seeking revenge against the country that he felt had betrayed him. Harp had apparently done it for profit.

Without looking, I could tell from the movement of the spar that Shayla had joined me. She sidled up next to me, reinforcing that our argument of a few hours past was over.

"It's written all over your face," she said.

I leaned back to take measure of her mood. "What is?"

"The schooner. You're like a boy looking at a new toy."

I wasn't about to deny it. In between trying to figure out Harp's game, I had thought of little else besides how the ship would handle the seas around the Horn. "Can't deny she's a beauty."

"One that we could make good use of," she said, then paused.

"Bloody cannibal!" Shayla spat out. "I'd take a piece of him as well, if I could. It'll be a long time before I forget that meal."

With her face reflecting the moonlight, I gazed on her beauty. There was no way, especially after our rough treatment earlier, that I would let her alone with him. "Not a chance."

"Is it your decision to make?" she asked.

I hadn't been delaying our nuptials on purpose, but they had not been a priority. We had escaped Cozumel with two of Lafitte's ships on our heels, and after leading them onto the reef in the Dry Tortugas, we had spent some time in Havana, as well as in a picturesque cove, where we had spent two weeks careening the ship. She knew any excuse I could muster for delaying our wedding would be badly played. She had me.

"Let's see what tomorrow brings." I wished then that we were married, but controlling her, if it could even be done, was not the right reason for our union. If I brought our wedding up now, it would be transparent, so I left it alone, promising myself it would become a priority.

Chapter 8

My thoughts turned from the schooner to the work that lay ahead. Diving had been much on my mind. With Mason a better navigator, and Rhames a superior warrior, I had time to explore the fascinating field. I'd had several ideas, but the bell we'd lost, especially after the improvements we made, had worked well enough. Even with all the churches scattered across Cuba, finding a suitable replacement would take time, if it was possible at all. A pile of gold was often not enough for the clergymen to part with their bells. Now, without one, I made a list of what I needed to make one of my ideas a reality.

What we had lacked in our underwater efforts was maneuverability. Limited by the capacity of our lungs, we could venture no farther from the bell's precious air supply than a short outgoing and return trip—often less than two minutes long, even for an experienced diver. When we had salvaged the *Wreck of the Ten Sail* we had fashioned rudimentary faceplates and wanted to improve on those efforts.

Combining the air supply of a bell and the range of the hose to create a faceplate that supplied air to the diver was my goal. In order to accomplish this we would need a sealant.

Looking over the rail at the multitude of pine trees that gave the island its name, I saw the source we needed. There had been no answer from Harp about our terms. Without one we would not be diving in the morning. With a day to prepare the headgear, and thinking we could hunt as well, I called for Blue. As usual he was bent over the rail with a line in his hand.

"Any luck?" I asked, noticing the bare deck beside him.

"Not a thing, Mr. Nick. Bottom is too sandy." He looked down at the deck in defeat.

"I'd like you to lead a hunting party to the island in the morning. We'll be needing to collect some pine sap as well." Blue's demeanor instantly changed, and when he looked up I could see the sparkle was back in his eyes.

"Is the bastard coming?" he inquired about Rhames.

With the lack of pirating, Rhames, Red, and Swift were often bored. Competitions often solved that problem. "How about you take one party and he another?" His expression became thoughtful.

"I'd hunt alone. Lucy can gather the pine sap." A smile broke his face.

After being awake the previous night, I was too exhausted to argue. Leaving it at that, I retired to a dreamless sleep.

———

IT WAS ALREADY LIGHT when I woke. Shayla was up and I quickly dressed and went on deck. Rhames, cutlass in hand, was on the foredeck guiding the freedmen through a series of maneuvers. After confirming there had been no message from Harp, I called him over and told him my plan. As I expected it was well received. "Take a few of the men if you like."

Rhames, Blue, Lucy, and two freedmen were quickly ready and loaded into the skiff. As the men pulled toward shore, I could hear the good-natured bantering between Rhames and

Blue. The words were soon lost over the water, but I was sure they were negotiating a wager. Turning away from them, I searched for Shayla. Finding her atop the rigging, I called for her to come down and told her my idea.

"A helmet of sailcloth with a porthole for a window? Are you daft?" She stood with her hands on hips.

"It'll work," I assured her. "Lucy has gone with the men to gather pine sap. We'll make it into pitch to seal everything." She didn't look confident, but I was determined. After explaining what I wanted her to fashion from our supply of sailcloth, I gathered the rest of the supplies. I soon had a small porthole, which I would pay a price for later when Shayla discovered it had come from our cabin, and a bucket.

Spreading the woodworking tools we had aboard on a hatch cover, I started to cut a hole the size of the porthole in the bucket. It was tedious work, having to drill several small holes then cutting out the wood between them. Once the rough work was done, I used the files and rasp to ease the edges and allow for a snug fit. Shayla had finished the sailcloth hood I asked for. Sliding it over the bucket I fit the porthole in, then cut the sailcloth around the inside, leaving enough extra to form a seal.

Lifting the contraption, the first thing I noticed was its weight. When underwater some heavy objects are lighter, and I hoped this would be the case with the helmet. As I slid it on, the immediate need for padding for the crown of my head became apparent, but more importantly, I was able to see out the porthole. With that accomplished, I had to figure out how to get the air hoses inserted, and how to seal the sailcloth now hanging loose around my shoulders. By now most of the crew were watching us, and, lifting the helmet from my head, I saw the divers in the group had stepped forward, clearly interested.

I explained the need for the air hoses and seal. All but one shook their heads, but the man I knew as James picked up the helmet and examined it, then set it down.

"How do we breathe?" he asked.

I knew James to be handy and took him below to disassemble one of our pumps. With the parts in hand, we brought them up to the deck, where we decided on the best location on the helmet to install the inlet. It would have to be drilled through the bucket using the thru-hull fittings we had removed from the discharge line from our pump. It was dark by the time I was ready to assemble the unit, and I looked toward the island to see how our hunters and Lucy had done.

A fire raged down the shore from where the skiff was beached. That told me at least one of the parties had success. Realizing I hadn't heard a shot fired, I guessed it was Blue. With his tracking ability and silent blowgun it appeared he'd bested the louder, better-armed pirate. I was happy for Blue, and knew his modesty belied his competitive nature. Once my eyes adjusted to the dark, I saw a smaller fire with a single figure beside it that looked like Lucy. The meat was important, but equally valuable was the pitch she was brewing.

An hour later they were back aboard. The hunters were boisterous as they unloaded the meat from a large boar. Blue's smile told me what I already expected. The crew gathered around Blue, but it was Lucy I needed, and with a tin bucket in hand she followed me to the hatch, where I had the materials spread out.

The wooden bucket Shayla had bolstered with old cloth was coated with lard before the sailcloth was smoothed over it. Next, I set the porthole over the hole, and, adding a bit of lard to the pine mixture to make it more pliable, rolled the pitch into a rope that I placed under and around the metal ring on the porthole. Using the screws I had extracted from the bulkhead earlier, I fastened the metal flange. This was as far as I dared to go before the pitch hardened.

The lookout called that a skiff was approaching, and gathering along the rail we eagerly waited for their answer to our terms. Harp had accepted and we confirmed that we would depart at daybreak. The mood turned boisterous. We might have been short on water, but the wine flowed. With the wind light and no other lights besides the schooner in sight, the crew celebrated the hunt and let off some steam. As the night wore on, I hoped the party would run its course and I wouldn't have to be the one to end it. We needed everyone aboard to have their wits about them in the morning. Fortunately, though a little later than I would have liked, the men started to amble around the deck looking for a suitable spot to spend the night. I watched carefully, my senses tuned into any sound that might be a man falling overboard.

Finally, near midnight, except for the chorus of snores, the deck was quiet. Once the wine was brought out, Shayla, Lucy, and I had decided to split the watch. I was just about to climb the mast and take station atop the spar when I heard a splash. Looking down on the deck, I counted bodies. With all the men accounted for, I started to climb the Jacob's ladder, but before I was even half-way up, I heard what sounded like someone floundering in the water.

Knowing I would have a better vantage point above, I continued climbing, but instead of looking up, I watched the deck and surrounding waters. Just as I thought I might have dreamed it, I saw the head of a man appear at the rail. A second later, he hoisted himself onto the deck. Cursing myself and the crew for leaving the ladder out, I quietly descended to meet him.

The man remained standing where he had broached the ship, seeming uncertain of his situation. His indecision didn't last long, though, and as I saw his head turn toward me, I recognized him as one of Harp's crew. Unarmed, I climbed around the mast, making as much noise as I could, trying to wake the men without appearing obvious. The wine held a firm embrace on them, and the snoring continued unabated. Not one moved.

Just as I extended my hands straight out to show the intruder that I was weaponless, I saw a shadow move behind him. A diminutive figure I instantly recognized as Lucy stepped out of the shadow. Before I could react, she had her blowgun to her mouth, and a second later the man fell to the deck.

Chapter 9

The ship fell silent. Even the snoring seemed to stop for a long second before it resumed. Slowly, Lucy and I approached the body. His motive unknown and fearing the crew might take retribution on him for Red and Swift's captivity, my first thought was to get him off the deck before anyone woke and saw him. Dragging the limp, wet body to the companionway, I called down to Shayla for help.

"He dead?"

"No. Lucy shot him with one of her darts. Help me get him to the cabin before he comes to."

With the two women's help I dragged him to our cabin, and rolled him through the door. By the time Lucy had bound his wrists and ankles, he was starting to wake up.

"What the bleedin' hell?" He struggled against the bonds, then realizing his fate, looked at us in turn, studying our faces.

"I'm the captain, Nick Van Doren. This is Shayla and Lucy."

"There's no need for all this. I was just paying my respects."

"That's an odd way of visiting—unannounced and past midnight."

"William Beauchamp, second lieutenant Royal Marines, at your service." He extended his bound hands as if this alone should ensure his release.

"Well, Mr. Beauchamp, before we release you, would you explain your clandestine visit?" Bare-chested and dressed in wet knickers, his look and gentrified voice were the only proof he could offer. "And why swim here? Very suspicious circumstances … don't you agree?"

"I meant to warn you. Harp has doubled the watch since spotting you. I had to sneak off."

His self-stated standing with the Royal Marines was curious aboard what I had at first taken as an escort ship.

"We suspected something was amiss on our visit."

"Amiss is a bit mild. Harp has renounced his commission and taken the ship."

That might explain why he was flying Swiss colors and was anchored in this remote backwater. "You'll have to give me more than that before we cut you loose."

"Our orders were to escort the sugar merchants through the Straits of Florida. We were successful, but Harp and the commodore of our fleet seldom saw eye to eye. Harp wanted to reap some of the rewards for our efforts, but the commodore would have none of it. Seeing those riches pass by enraged Harp. That and his condition."

Shayla was unusually quiet, and when I glanced over at her, I saw her face was flushed and her eyes fixed on Beauchamp. Thinking Beauchamp's presence was as much a curse as a blessing, I reached into my locker, grabbed the largest shirt I had, and tossed it to him. He caught it with his bound hands and shrugged. Beauchamp's story confirmed my own theory, but I kept my guard up.

"What do you want of us?"

"I'd like to see Harp hanged myself, but I'd be grateful if you'd drop me at your next port."

He was obviously unaware of our own dubious standing. I nodded to Lucy, who cut Beauchamp's ties.

"Think it's the truth?" Shayla asked, her attention temporarily diverted from the officer.

"No reason to doubt him. Not that I'd trust him. Could be a ruse by Harp to infiltrate our crew." I had no issue talking in front of him.

"I'd think he'd send a seaman if that were his aim. Someone that we would take right in and who would blend with the crew."

She was right. Onboard a ship, the crew knew everything that went on.

Beauchamp rubbed his wrists, looking around for what I guessed was a weapon if things went badly.

"I'd be careful with the Africans if I was you," I warned him. "It was her dart that took you down coming over the rail." While Beauchamp put the shirt on, I thought that Lucy and Blue might be the least of his trouble. When Rhames woke up and found out he was aboard, there was sure to be a pissing match.

"I'd rather take my chances with your lot than Harp. He's a bit unglued."

I couldn't dispute that comment. From what I'd seen of Harp earlier, he was exactly the sort who would denounce his commission and take to piracy. It might have been the syphilis or something else I had seen in men like him: a driving force that ended up getting them, as well as their followers, killed.

"I'll have to meet with my crew." I didn't want him to know I had sole authority in this matter, at least not yet. "Best make yourself comfortable until I give the all-clear signal. Lucy will keep you company until then." Lucy raised the blowgun from her lap, and blew into the tube. Beauchamp flinched, but it was empty. Removing a dart from her bag, she set it on the table as a warning, and smiled.

I made to leave the cabin, expecting Shayla to be right behind me, but she lingered for a minute before entering the passageway. Holding my tongue, I climbed the stairs to the companionway, grateful for the fresh air on deck. With several hours until dawn, and the deck scattered with sleeping men, I climbed back into the rigging.

A few minutes later I felt Shayla next to me on the top spar. We had spent enough time together on the thin piece of wood that our feet found their usual holds, but I sensed a distance between us. She appeared deep in thought. As I gazed across the water at the schooner, now swathed in darkness, I wondered how Beauchamp's disappearance would affect the ship.

"We should keep him below. Only trouble will come if Harp finds out he's aboard."

"Rhames as well."

"Keeping secrets from the crew rarely turns out well."

She was of course right, but I meant the subterfuge to last only the day. The feasibility of salvaging the wreck would determine how we played our hand. "Just until we see how things shake out today."

We stayed aloft until the first rays of dawn lit the sky. The sunrise showed only a few pink streaks, indicating fair weather. Someone moved below and I glanced down to see the figure of a man in the companionway. The sky had just started to lighten, but the deck was still dark and for a brief second I thought it was Beauchamp, but it turned out to be Mason. He'd partaken as much as the next man in the past night's festivities, and rubbed his eyes as he looked around the deck and then over the water.

With a grin on his face, he rang the bell, waking the men

on deck. Slowly the ship came to life beneath us, and I climbed back down to face the day.

From across the water came the sound of the chain rode being hauled aboard as the schooner weighed anchor. "Right, then. Shake those cobwebs out and we'll get on with it." The men moved slowly at first, but once Rhames gained his wits, he drove them hard. The schooner slid past us just as our sails filled with the morning breeze and we followed her out of the bay.

It was a short trip to the bank. As we approached I left Mason in command and went below. Beauchamp was sitting at my desk with a plate of pork in front of him. Cleaning her fingernails with the sharp point of a dart, Lucy sat on the bunk watching him.

"What can you tell me about the wreck by the bank?" I asked Beauchamp, not trusting Harp's story of how it got there.

He took one more bite before putting down the fork. "She's Spanish. A merchant ship that refused Harp's command to heave to and be boarded. He meant to fire a warning shot at her, but the aim was off and we sank her."

Chapter 10

With both ships moving out there was time to ask Beauchamp about what he knew of the current political climate. Wanting to appear cooperative he started his narrative at the end of the war between the British and Americans more than a decade ago, North American seas, including the Caribbean, had been quiet. Spain, still busy trying to suppress insurgencies in her diminishing empire, was no longer the threat she once was. Spanish efforts were currently centered around quelling the Mexican rebellion. The Napoleonic wars were over, leaving the continent quiet, and that peace extended to the European holdings in the Caribbean.

With no privateering commissions available except for the Mexican province of Campeche, whose flag Lafitte was currently flying, a British deserter would be labeled a pirate, which only made Harp's decisions even more curious. The only explanation for his actions that made sense was his sickness. Even this attempt to recover whatever he'd lost off the *Banco de San Antonio* was reckless. Cuba, as the closest Spanish holding to Mexico, had a continuous stream of boat traffic between the island and the mainland. It occurred to me that it might have been a Spanish ship, trying to evacuate whatever treasure was left in their coffers from the rebel state. Broke and desperate, Spain would take every ounce of gold or silver it could.

The schooner passed our bow, bringing me back to reality. She unfurled her sails and I couldn't help but notice that I wasn't the only one aboard who watched her as she picked up speed and danced through the waves. Mason called out for all sail, but it took everything we had to keep the schooner in sight.

Leaving the rail, I moved toward the binnacle, where Mason was studying a chart. I, as well as everyone aboard, knew he had them committed to memory, but ever-cautious he double-checked the soundings being called from the bow against the chart.

"No need to push. We know where they're headed."

Mason looked up. "Reckless, if you ask me."

"Yes," I agreed, and thinking about with whom and where we were headed, I called for Rhames.

"We should get the guns ready. There's something about this business that's not right."

"Aye, we've got a knack for finding trouble, don't we?" He grinned. "The boys can use the practice. We'll be ready."

I left Rhames to his guns and Mason at the helm. Gathering the divers, we went forward to assemble the equipment. The pitch had dried overnight into a hard but pliable sealant. Testing the headgear, I placed the bucket over my head and after several adjustments felt reasonably comfortable. I knew once in the water the buoyancy would ease the pressure on the crown of my head.

"How do we seal the bottom?" one of the men asked.

We'd stopped work before solving the problem last night.

Water could easily find its way through the flaps from the sail-cloth draped over my chest and flood the helmet. I took it off and asked one of the other men to wear it. Weight seemed to be the answer, and I called Shayla and Lucy to sew some pieces of lead around the edge. It would still leak, but with the positive pressure from the incoming air, the facial area should stay clear at least that's what I thought. The only way to find out would be to get in the water.

The excitement I felt about testing the new gear and the rumble of the guns being run into their ports below my feet overcame my concern for Harp. Just as Shayla and Lucy finished sewing the lead into the flaps, I heard Mason call to the men in the rigging.

He ordered several sheets released and half our sails fell to the spars where the men quickly lashed them. With the triangular-shaped foresails pushing us forward, we crept up on the bank. Harp's ship lay directly ahead and we could clearly hear the sound of the anchor and chain as it dropped to the bottom. The foresails allowed us to sail close to the wind, and we were soon anchored a few dozen yards off Harp's port side.

"I'm going up to have a look," I told Mason.

Rhames stopped me before I started my climb. "We're ready if the bastards are up to no good. If it weren't for my boys, Red and Swift, I'd blow the bastards right now."

I almost told him about our guest. A few minutes with Rhames and we would know the truth about Harp as well as Beauchamp's motive. It would have to wait, though, as I wanted all hands and eyes on deck. Reaching the top spar, I called out to the other lookouts to keep an eye on the horizon. Harp needed us, but another passing ship, especially if she were Spanish or British, might be a problem.

Shading my eyes from the glare coming off the water, I peered into its depths. From this height, I could see the dark outline of the reef. The individual features were hidden, but as I scanned the perimeter where the coral heads dropped to the sand, I thought I saw the straight lines that told me we were on the wreck.

"Bring her up twenty yards," I yelled down to Mason, who relayed the order to the men at the capstan. Slowly they brought in the chain, and when the stern was directly over the wreck I called for them to stop. We would still work off the skiff, but now we could do so with it tied off to the ship, something that gave me some comfort if we needed to leave in a hurry.

Climbing back down, I could barely contain my excitement, but knew I had to wear the stone face of a captain. Once the work was over and we were safe I would let down my guard, but not before.

"Right, then. Let's get the gear loaded and see what we've got." The divers gathered and carried the helmet, pumps, and hoses to the skiff. Once everything was loaded, and with two men aboard to man the oars, we swung the davits overboard and lowered it. When the skiff was released the men rowed to the stern, where Mason had lines waiting. After securing the boats, I dropped the rope ladder and was about to climb overboard when I felt a hand grab my arm. From the touch I knew it was Shayla.

"Don't be thinking that you're going to test that wig."

It was exactly what I planned to do. "Just up and down. I'll have two freedivers with me." I knew she didn't like it, but I was determined.

Standing with her hands on her hips, she stared me down as I placed the cloth-clad bucket over my head. With one leg over the side, I made sure one of the men was ready to guide the hoses and gave a thumbs-up to the two men in the water.

Just as I was about to submerge, a blast of warm air blew into the helmet. It had a slight taste of the whale oil we used to lubricate the pump. Hanging onto the side, I started breathing. It was an awkward feeling, exhaling at the same time as the fresh air entered the chamber, but the excess quickly found the gaps in the lead sewn into the cloth resting on my shoulders. I took my time acclimating to the gear and after several minutes I was comfortable enough to release my grip.

The first mistake became evident as I fought to submerge. The weight sewn into the sailcloth seemed to accomplish its primary purpose, but wasn't enough to compensate for the extra buoyancy of the air-filled bucket. I had no choice but to ascend. Once my head broke the surface, the weight of the gear took me back under. Fortunately, one of the free divers had seen my struggle and surfaced with me.

He called out for more weight, and taking a bag of shot in each hand, I quickly sank. Silt rose from the sandy bottom when I hit reducing the visibility. I waited, breathing deeply and regularly until it cleared. The gear appeared to work flawlessly, with the only problem being fog on the glass. The cause of which I guessed was the contrast of the warm, humid air being pumped into the helmet and the cool seawater on either side of the glass.

If that was our biggest problem the test was a grand success. The silt had settled and I scanned my surroundings through the hazy glass. By twisting my head slightly, I was able to see through a clear area of the porthole. The feeling of standing on the bottom of the sea, thirty-odd feet under the surface, and breathing clean air was almost overwhelming. As I made my way toward the reef, I watched as the free divers made several trips to the surface and back.

The wreck lay ahead, but as I walked toward it a jerk halted my progress. Turning back, I realized I had reached the end of the hose. In order to explore the wreck further the skiff would have to be freed from the ship in order to stay above the diver. It was another small problem, but one I couldn't immediately communicate to the support divers.

With my limited mobility I only was able to reach the transom of the ship. She appeared to be a brigantine, similar to our own. Green slime had already started the process of turning the hull into a reef, but she was fresh in the water, and from the look of her, not a sugar trader.

Chapter 11

STEVEN BECKER

UNCHARTED

Waters

Just as I recovered from the first pull of the hose, my head jerked backwards, causing me to lose my footing. Regaining my balance, I realized I was being dragged back to the skiff, but before I could return on my own the line jerked again. Pain shot through my neck, and not sure what was happening other than I was being recalled, I started a lumbering pace across the bottom to allow some slack in the line. Ahead I saw one of the freedivers signaling me up.

Dropping the weights and assisted by the buoyancy of the air in the helmet, I was soon floundering on the surface. Underwater the weight of the gear was almost imperceptible; out of the water it was a different matter. I fought to stay afloat while my eyes acclimated to the sun. To make matters worse, the porthole was now covered in condensation. I heard voices calling my name, and then a shot fired.

The shot was close enough I assumed it to be from one of our guns. A few seconds later another gun fired, this one clearly further away. A large splash nearby threw up a wake that took me under. Disoriented, I fought for the surface. Hands grabbed me under each arm as the men above tried to

57

assist me. Breaking through the surface again, those same hands struggled to remove the helmet. Pain shot through my neck each time they pulled and I quickly realized that what they were attempting was futile. Something had happened to the headgear. I broke free and signaled that I was going to descend.

Void of sight, I inverted my body in an attempt to relieve the pressure on my neck. The acrobatics freed whatever was stuck and the helmet dropped off. My lungs burned and, now unencumbered by the gear, I pushed to the surface. Squinting into the sun I found myself in a full-on naval battle.

My sight had returned but the scene was obscured. Cannon thundered from our ship and our unknown foe remained invisible behind a curtain of smoke. Treading water, I spun around and suddenly saw the bow of the skiff appear through the haze. Men were calling my name and I realized they were searching for me.

The skiff slid back into the haze. "Over here!" I called out, then realized even if they could hear me, with clouds of black smoke floating around us they wouldn't know where the call was from.

"Back-paddle," I ordered, and when the stern appeared, I called out for them to turn toward port. The smoke soon lifted enough for them to see and I was aboard in short order with two very scared men and Blue.

"What happened?" I asked as I scanned the water. Shots continued and the smoke wafted back and forth, giving the scene a surreal look.

"Spanish. Two frigates opened fire on us."

"Where's Harp?"

"Bastard ran."

I often thought Blue's use of Rhames's vernacular amusing, but not in this case. "Can you find the reef?" Unable to determine what was happening around us, that was the safest place for the small, unarmed skiff. If our enemy wasted a shot at us we would be a small target and the reef would protect us from any pursuit.

Blue called to the two freedmen at the oars, who understood the urgency behind his order. They needed no prodding, only direction, and pulled hard for the safety of the *Banco de San Antonio*. Coral heads soon became visible beneath us, some appearing to reach within inches of the shallow-draft skiff. Once we were safely ensconced within its borders, I called for the oars to be shipped and turned back to the battle.

The guns had ceased firing and the smoke cleared, revealing three ships: two frigates and our brigantine. My heart dropped when I saw grappling hooks cross our rail. The lines went tight as the Spanish crew pulled the larger frigate alongside. Smoke rose from our ship, but it still looked to be intact. One of the masts was askew, its rigging hanging into the water, and from the attitude of the ship it appeared she was taking on water.

Once our ship was secured, the other frigate moved off in pursuit of a small shape on the horizon. Harp was running hard to the south. Rhames would have seen our ship's destiny as soon as the grappling hooks caught our rail and I could only hope he would surrender rather than fight a pitched battle against a superior force. Drifting on the current, we sat and watched as our crew surrendered and was taken aboard the frigate. Blue was close to me and I could see the anxious look on his face that mirrored mine.

"Bastards," he muttered under his breath when he saw Lucy and Shayla forced aboard the Spanish ship.

"At least they're alright. We'll get them," I tried to reassure him but, as I saw Shayla pushed across the gangplank set between the two ships, I was worried for all of them. The only hope for their well-being was the man standing on the quarterdeck. From his attire I guessed he was the captain. His control over his crew would make him my friend until we had a plan to rescue them—then he would be my enemy.

Counting heads as they crossed to the Spanish frigate, several men appeared to have minor injuries, but they were all accounted for. Once they were aboard they were herded through the companionway and disappeared below. I continued to watch as a dozen or so Spanish men dragged two heavy ropes across. Again, the captain had proven to be my ally. In attempting to save the ship, he was keeping our treasure from the grasp of the sea.

Once the salvage operation was underway, I turned to Blue and the two men at the oars. "We need to get out of here while they're occupied."

Isle de los Pinos was the closest refuge and I took a bearing on the sun before giving the men a heading. It wasn't difficult with the shoreline in sight. Sweat flowed from the foreheads of the freedmen at the oars as they fought against the strong current running through the channel. When we reached the southern side of the point, I called for a break. Blue and I changed places with the men to take our turn and we soon spotted the island.

I had hoped, but had not expected, to see a mast in the bay. Harp had run south, but with the Spanish frigate in chase, I assumed he was making for the safety of the smaller Cayman Islands. News of his mutiny might have reached the governor's ears in Grand Cayman, but the smaller islands' residents would likely be ignorant of Harp's new status as a pirate. I only hoped Swift and Red would remain alive until we could rescue the crew, find a ship, and save them. Schooner or not, I would have my revenge against Harp.

The water changed shades from a light, almost-translucent blue to a deep, dark indigo as we left the shelter of the point. Fighting the current running across the mouth of the bay, Blue and I pulled hard, finally collapsing on our oars as we reached its protection. Gasping huge gulps of air, we surveyed the water behind us for any sign of pursuit. For now we were alone.

Now that we were inside the shallow bay, the current eased, allowing us to make good progress. Bypassing the anchorage that Harp had used, we continued to the east. I wanted to find refuge somewhere out of sight of the shipping lanes and close to the mainland to facilitate our rescue attempt. Facing the stern I was able to watch for any pursuit. For the time being, we appeared to be safe and my thoughts turned to Shayla, Lucy, and the men. Havana was the likely port where the Spanish would have taken the ship and crew. With protected deepwater anchorages, the city housed the ever-present Spanish bureaucracy. It was my opinion that if the captain expected reward, he would head there.

"There's a good landing. Good hunting and fresh water." Blue pointed to a copse of palms set against a black-sand beach.

Changing course, we headed toward the small cove. By the time we hauled the skiff onto the beach the sun was sinking in the west. We were tired from the escape, but I could feel the tension running through Blue and myself as we stood on the fine, volcanic sand. It was only natural to want to get right to it, but with no weapons and just four men, we would have to be smart about our plan. For now, we needed provisions and rest.

Putting aside my emotions, I tried to think things through. "With the ship in tow, and assuming they are heading for Havana, they won't reach the harbor until morning." I said it to rationalize my decision as well as for Blue's benefit.

"Right, Mr. Nick. We'll get the bastards in the morning."

"And our women."

He nodded. Hauling the skiff above the high-water mark took the rest of our energy and the four of us collapsed on the beach. We rested until just before dark when Blue came alert. He had sensed something and I slowly lifted myself up to scan the bush behind us. The setting sun reflected a dozen pair of eyes staring back at me.

"We can't fight them," I said, standing with my hands held high. The crew followed my example and we were soon surrounded by a group of natives.

Chapter 12

Despite popular myths, island natives are not always hostile. Considering our own outlaw status, we, too, were often enemies of the governments we found ourselves entangled with. This made for some strange alliances, but being close to Spanish soil, I hoped the men approaching us could be convinced we were friends. With bows drawn and the tips of their arrows held steady, the group emerged from the bush. I tried to stay optimistic. Surely, this close to Cuba, and with the Spaniards' proclivity toward enslaving anyone they could capture to keep the sugar plantations producing, the men standing before me had to be the enemy of my enemy—and therefore my friends

Three men advanced under the watchful eyes and arrows of the rest of the party. One man greeted me in a language that sounded familiar, but I didn't understand. Shayla was our translator, though thankfully Blue, too, had a knack for native dialects. This one seemed to be a mix between the indigenous Carib and the slaves' native tongues, and Blue understood enough to communicate. He and the man exchanged a few words, then an unassuming figure made his way through the group.

It appeared the natives disguised their chiefs as we did our captains. He came forward under the protection of several men, and lifted a hand. At first I thought it was the signal to fire, then he leveled his palm at his waist and motioned to the ground. The men obeyed and lowered their weapons.

Relief spread through us and I thought that if the chief had revealed himself then I should as well. Extending a hand toward him, in the manner the American president Thomas Jefferson had made fashionable, I greeted him.

With his warriors still wary behind him, the chief and Blue spoke for the next few minutes. There was quite a bit of head-nodding from the men within earshot, which I took to be a good sign. After more talk, Blue followed him through the copse of palm trees and waved back to me and the two freedmen, indicating we should follow.

The terrain quickly rose as we left the black-sand beach. Pine trees replaced the palms near the beach as we gained elevation. We were quiet as we walked, still tired after our escape, and when we reached the camp, perched near the top of a hill, we collapsed by a small fire. Thirsty, I drank deeply from the skins that were distributed, thankfully with fresh water and not wine or spirits. After we drank our fill and recovered, I rose and looked around.

Over the last few years we had been both guests and prisoners in several native villages. This one was well laid out and nicely organized, a neat and business-like affair. With the three-hundred-sixty-degree view offered by the summit, it was no wonder they had spotted us. The village was situated among several peaks, some larger and many smaller, all covered with pine trees. The valleys below held lakes and streams. There was little in the way of arable land needed by the plantations;

as such, deemed not "profitable" it was probably the reason the village existed.

We were fed and allowed to rest until dark, then around the glow of a bonfire the villagers assembled and started asking questions. Blue had a grasp on their language, but it was far from a fluid conversation. Adding hand signals whenever I could to help clarify our situation, they seemed to understand, and to my relief, appeared sympathetic.

Now that we knew they were friendly, the question was, would they help us? Speaking to Blue, who sat by my side, we agreed it was time to ask for their help. He made a request and immediately heads started to shake back and forth. There was no need for an interpreter.

I felt the weight of the small pouch I'd carried to Harp's ship yesterday against my hip. "Maybe a little gold'll change things," I said to Blue.

I thought if I whispered to Blue it would seem devious, and so was speaking to him in a normal voice, assuming they didn't understand. But at the mention of gold, I could see from their faces, lit by the flames from the fire, that they knew the word.

From my earlier survey of Cuba, I'd observed none of the rock formations or rivers where gold was usually found; this didn't mean there wasn't any here, of course. Columbus had discovered the island almost three-hundred years ago, and rumors persisted that he'd left behind a secret gold mine. This I doubted.

It was too late to undo what my outspoken words had done; my only option was to make the best of it. Removing the pouch from my britches, I released the drawstring attached to my belt, and emptied the coins onto the ground. The group drew closer, in awe of what they conceived as unfathomable wealth. One at a time, I picked up the coins and replaced them in the pouch. I didn't put it away, though; I wanted them to know it could be theirs.

"Let's start with needing weapons and a guide," I told Blue.

The conversation turned into a negotiation, and though there were sometimes raised voices and looks of disgust and disbelief on both Blue and the chief's faces, I knew this was stagecraft.

Suddenly both men looked at me.

"Three coins, Mr. Nick," Blue said.

Wanting to show the chief that Blue had the authority to strike a deal, I handed him the pouch, showing the chief that Blue was my equal. The chief smiled as Blue carefully extracted three coins from the pouch, then tucked it away.

"Four guns, ammunition, and a guide," Blue told me, after handing the coins to the chief.

I could see the look of respect for my compatriot on the chief's face, and the frequent glances toward me that he had cast during the first round of the negotiations stopped. From the puffed-up chest and look on Blue's face, I could tell he was enjoying his new status.

"We'll need provisions and more men," I said, thinking if the Spanish had taken the women and crew to Havana, we would be facing at least a garrison.

Blue spoke to the chief, then turned to me. "We should travel light. It is a long row across the bay, then two days' march to Havana. Less if we can find horses."

I knew Blue would rather walk than ride, but there was an urgency to the situation. Our men were likely to be enslaved; there was no telling what would happen to the women. Despite his distaste for horses, there was no doubt that Blue would ride almost anything to save Lucy.

The mood lightened and fresh skins were passed around. These contained some kind of sweet liquor, and I cautioned myself and my men to moderation. An hour later, after taking only small sips, I could feel my head spin. Seeking a secluded place, I lay down and shut my eyes.

Chapter 13

Activity around the camp woke me before dawn. As I got up, I could feel yesterday's exertion in my muscles and joints, but I was determined to get Shayla and the crew back, not to mention the treasure aboard the ship.

I had formed an attachment to both our previous ships, the *Panther* and the *Cayman*. Both were named for animals that we had fought along our journeys: panthers in the Everglades and crocodiles on Grand Cayman. Like a child with his first toys, they were important to me, but with both lost—one through a trade, and the other through the deception of Emanuel, the man who had led us to Henriques's cache in Cozumel—I had a different, more detached opinion of our transport now.

The ship didn't matter; the treasure aboard did. The silver bars recovered from the *Wreck of the Ten Sail*, and the gold from our adventure in Haiti were hard-fought prizes. Rescuing the crew had priority, but I had no intention of leaving Cuba broke. Getting up, I found Blue and the freedmen eating by the fire. Though I was anxious to get started, I knew I needed to eat. We finished the meal and were preparing to depart when the chief came over and introduced our guide.

I was surprised, though I shouldn't have been. The man was clearly a Spaniard, but his long, scraggly beard and uncut hair told me he had been exiled here. It wasn't unusual to find expats in the Caribbean. There were any number of circumstances, be it shipwrecks, escaped prisoners, or even disease such as Harp suffered, that could push a man to the outskirts of civilization. I greeted him in Spanish, and was again surprised when he returned the salutation in English.

"Good day to ya, Captain."

"Nick Van Doren." I rose and extended my hand. The calluses I felt told me he was a worker, and looking into his eyes, I saw the whites were clear—both good signs, though he did have an edge about him.

"Juan de Cordova."

"Glad to have you aboard. Are you aware of our circumstances?"

"The chief told me your women and crew were taken."

"Pardon my inquiry," I started, wanting to know at least something of his history. There were too many similarities with Emanuel. "You're Spanish, yet—"

"I was Spanish," he cut me off. "Just a name now."

His explanation was cut short by Blue coming up behind us. He nodded to the horizon, where I saw the first rays of light breaking over the water. Part one of our plan required an early morning departure in order to utilize the glare of the rising sun to disguise our transit across the bay, as well as avoid the afternoon winds and heat. Juan's story would have to wait.

"Right, then. Are the men ready?"

Blue nodded, and handed me a rifle. Taking it by the barrel, the first thing I noticed was the rust covering the metal. Scolding myself for sleeping instead of servicing our newly purchased weapons, I could only hope that the rest of the weapon was in better condition than its surface. It was a battle in these climes to keep the rust at bay, but one that needed to be fought.

"Ammunition?" I asked Blue, who handed me a pouch that I guessed from its weight contained a few dozen rounds. Not nearly enough if we were forced into a fight. "That's it?"

"He says they have no more."

I cursed again. My diligence had been lax and I hoped we wouldn't pay a price for it. There was no point harping on it now. I attached the pouch to my belt and prepared to move out. The other men had rifles as well. Blue also had one and his blow gun. Starting down the hill, we quickly reached the bay.

Our skiff remained where we had left it, and after a brief inspection, we loaded the provisions we had bargained for and pushed off the beach. The water was dark and the sky speckled with stars. Only a sliver of light showed in the eastern sky as we set the oars into their locks. The freedmen silently placed the blades in the water.

The chief had been correct and the crossing was an arduous task. I was glad for our early start when the wind came up, but we were close to shore by the time the waves started to whitecap. Our plan appeared to have succeeded, at least to this point. Juan had chosen an isolated stretch of mangrove-covered shoreline to land. The beach might have been easier, but easy wasn't often the best way. Wasting no time, as soon as we hit the shallows, we jumped from the skiff and, fighting through the muck, hauled the boat into the brush.

Though we wanted a rest, the conditions along the shore were inhospitable. Trying to ignore the swarming mosquitoes, we pushed through the tangled branches and roots. It seemed like a mile, but was likely only a hundred yards when we broke through into a clearing. Judging from the size and cultivation of the field, we found ourselves on the outskirts of a sugar plantation. Unfortunately, the harvest had been completed, and instead of having the cover of the large stalks, we were exposed.

"We need to move around the perimeter," Juan said, as he set out toward a small forested rise in the otherwise flat landscape.

In single file, with Juan leading and Blue trailing, covering our tracks as went, we moved toward the trees. Save for the iguanas snacking on the downed stalks, we were alone as we made our way through the fallow field. After climbing the rise, the plantation spread out below. The main house was clearly visible in a clearing laid out with a half-dozen buildings of different sizes and functions. I guessed at what must have been the foreman's house, school house, kitchens, smokehouse, work-shops, and slave quarters.

These buildings held little interest to us. Off to the side I noticed a large open-air structure housing the boiling vats for the cane. Huge piles of stalks were piled nearby, with what appeared to be all hands preparing the crop. On the outskirts I could see several men with rifles watching the operation. It was an area we wanted to avoid, but beyond it lay the stables—and the horses.

With no cover between us and the processing area, we would be exposed for a hundred yards, unless we backtracked and skirted the entire plantation. That might have made sense, except that there could just as easily have been other, unknown obstacles to face.

Deciding we were too close to our goal to turn back, we discussed splitting up and walking separately toward the stables. The thought proved unnerving to the freedmen, who if seen would be assumed to be runaway slaves and punished accordingly. After observing the goings-on for a few minutes, I realized that role-playing might be the answer. A man acting like a slave that belonged there would not be questioned.

Juan and I rubbed dirt on our exposed skin. It served to

darken our appearance, as well as lighten the mood a little. The freedmen took over now, knowing exactly what to do. Backtracking down the rise, we scoured the picked field for enough stalks to appear that we were completing the harvest, picked them up, and started toward the stables.

We made it to the processing building, where we switched the stalks to our shoulders facing the work party and continued unquestioned. Once around the corner we dropped the stalks and ran for the stables. Without knowing if anyone was inside, we moved single file to the door, where Blue peered inside. He waved us off, and instead of entering we moved along the exterior of the building to an open-air walkway.

Stalls lined both sides of the breezeway. Half were empty, the others occupied by horses crunching hay. Ducking into an empty stall, we waited while Blue scouted the area. He returned a few minutes later giving the all-clear sign.

"Right, then. Can you all ride?" I asked.

"Only been in the back of a wagon, Captain," one of the freedmen said.

The other nodded. Blue was not fond of the animals either, and when horses were involved, fear on the part of the rider was a problem. With three out of five of us unsure about riding, our best option was to take a carriage.

Finding and negotiating with the owner or foreman would be risky. There was no way of predicting their allegiance or their willingness to sell us a horse and wagon. I didn't want to steal either, but we had no option. The next hurdle to overcome was finding a rig, but we were lucky, and on exiting the breezeway found two horses harnessed to a ten-foot open wagon.

Another stroke of luck befell us when a bell clanged and the men and women working the plantation started toward the kitchens. We waited until the last strangler had passed and ran for the wagon. Juan and I hopped onto the driver's seat, while Blue and the two freedmen jumped in the back.

With a low whistle and a smack of the reins, Juan got the attention of the horses, who slowly dropped the stalks of hay they were chewing and started down the path.

Chapter 14

As the miles passed beneath us, I started to become more confident. It was late afternoon and there were a few other parties on the road. We felt quite a bit of trepidation as the first few groups passed, but whether it was riders in a group or a driver and a wagon, each offered only salutations. It finally occurred to me that with the freedmen in back we looked the part of traveling landowners. After a time, Juan started to speak to the passing travelers. I understood enough Spanish to ascertain that we were at least on the correct road to Havana.

I heard the Spanish word for forty, *caurenta*, several times. I was used to estimating speed over water, not land, but, figuring we were making between three and four miles per hour, we would have to find a place to overnight. Traveling these roads after dark was a dangerous business. We were tired from the crossing and the sun was starting to dip low in the west when I asked Juan to find us a suitable camping spot.

I saw a plantation ahead. "How about there?"

"Best to pull off the road. Too many questions there."

He was right. The lure of a hot meal and bed had gotten to me. Putting comfort from my mind, I asked Blue to search the road ahead for a suitable campsite. Juan was initially against the idea of Blue going scouting, but when he saw the pygmy blend into the scenery, he relented. It wasn't a half-hour later that he returned.

"Up ahead. There's a dirt road where we can pull the wagon off and some rocks that'll give us cover."

We followed him to the turnoff, where he then fell behind us, using the stiff fronds from a palmetto tree to erase any evidence of our passing. The road ended in a near-perfect spot —almost too much so. We were still in the valley, but to the north I could see the hills of an inland range. It was nothing like we had climbed in Haiti, but at the base of the foothills, the rocks allowed us to pull the wagon into a narrow cut, making it invisible even if someone should find the path.

We sat back, eating and drinking our dwindling provisions, as Juan had hobbled the horses and released them nearby to nibble the thick grass. As the dark of night set in, our exhaustion lulled us into a state of laziness. Our small group rested our backs against the rock outcropping that hid our wagon. It was an easily defensible space—although one I should have investigated further.

Twilight is fleeting in the tropics, and with the darkness our senses became fine-tuned to our surroundings. Nocturnal predators become active and I could hear several small animals scavenging nearby. Blue left to check on some snares he had set earlier after discovering the small-game trails running through the area.

When the horses spooked I knew what I'd missed. I'd made the mistake of trusting our position and not posting a watch. If I had pictured our camp as a ship, I would have insisted we take the higher ground. Now, looking up, I saw the silhouettes of two men atop one of the taller rocks. They were looking down at us. When I saw one raise his rifle, I called out to Juan and the freedmen, who found cover before the shot was fired.

I was not so lucky. Closest to the men above, I was still exposed and running for a rock to shield me when I felt something strike my calf. It was hot as an iron, but not debilitating, and I was able to hobble behind the rocks. Our group was in a state of confusion. Used to the confines of a ship, where each man had an assigned station, the fluid openness of the site worked against us.

"Over here! Bring the horse," I called out to the men, who had scattered following the shots. Juan and the freedmen answered my call, and were soon by my side, but none was willing to brave the open pasture to secure the horse. This was a concern, but not urgent, as the men above us would steal them before they killed them. Conversely, we would be shot first.

"Can you see anyone else?" I asked. Peering around the corner of the rock, I assigned each man to a compass point. At least with the outcropping at our backs we would see anyone approach.

"You're hit, Captain," one of the freedmen said.

I looked down at the blood streaming from the wound. This wasn't my first injury, or even the first bullet I had taken. The scars from the jaws of the panther that had attacked me in the Everglades were visible just above the bullet wound. "Keep watch."

Sitting on a small rock, I checked the wound, first to see if there was an exit hole. If the projectile had lodged itself within me, there was little chance I would keep the leg. Breathing a sigh of relief, I saw two holes. The bullet had gone sideways through the muscle behind my shin bone. The next order of business was to clean and bind the wound. Without the proper supplies, I tore a strip from my already ragged shirt, and tied it around my calf. The bleeding soon slowed to a trickle, then stopped altogether.

Looking around, I saw the two men were still high above

us. If there were any others nearby, I assumed they would have attacked, but, not knowing the extent of my injury or how well-armed we were, they kept their distance. It appeared to be a standoff, and I would have been happy to see them come to the same conclusion and leave, when one of the men suddenly dropped to the ground. The other bent over him, and looking around defensively, dragged him into a copse of pine trees.

Blue, who had been away from camp checking his snares, must have snuck up on them and shot the fallen man with his blowgun. I had no doubt Blue had the other in his sights. Now that they'd moved away, I had the confidence to scout the area.

"Juan, take Luis, and have a look back to the main road. Gabriel, you're with me."

We waited until the two men were further away, then Gabriel and I crossed back behind the rocks and checked the wagon. It appeared intact. Moving in increasingly larger circles, we scouted the entire area. Running into Juan and Luis, who had seen nothing on the road, I guessed the pair above us were alone.

Fighting the pain in my calf, I left Gabriel to guard the horses and, with Juan and Luis, climbed up to where Blue now had the two men under guard. He had several options in his array of darts, in addition to the poison ones that inflicted an immediate death. Blue had chosen one that merely knocked a man unconscious. The drugged man was coming to, but still groggy, when we reached them.

"Got the bastards, Mr. Nick."

Rhames would have been proud. I looked at the two men, trying to determine what they were about before I interrogated them. I often found that silence paid dividends as well and was in no rush.

"We meant no harm. Just after your horses is all," the taller man said.

"Just," I snarled.

Blue, sensing my distress, looked down and saw my bound leg. He dropped to one knee and unwrapped my makeshift bandage. As soon as he released the pressure, the blood flowed freely again.

"It's good for now," I said. I wasn't yet feeling light-headed or otherwise from the loss of blood and needed to keep my wits until this situation was handled. After Blue had retied the bandage, I stood and walked to the men.

"Just the horses." I repeated for them to understand it was as bad to steal a man's horses as it was to shoot him—and they had done both.

"What are we to make of you two?" I asked, hoping they would answer my questions without me having to interrogate them. I had learned that information was more reliable when given freely than when coerced. From the few sentences they had spoken, I had already learned they were British and an idea popped into my head.

"We's been on the run for the better part of a week. Ain't ate or drank nothing," the man who had spoken earlier said.

The other man was still under the influence of Blue's dart. What his companion had said about being on the run confirmed my previous thought.

"And what would you be on the run from?" I asked in the manner government officials usually ask questions—as if you were guilty.

"We was crew aboard a British ship. Something was amiss about the captain and me and my friend here, we swam to shore and been trying to reach Havana, figuring we can hop aboard another ship there."

"What do you know about this captain?" I didn't want to let on I knew who it was.

"Crazy was he. Deserter, pirate, whatever." He paused. "What we ate ..." He left the rest for our imagination.

Chapter 15

They had my sympathy and, trying to appear friendly, I lowered my hands and signaled for the men to drop their weapons. "We're headed to Havana if you'd like to join us."

"Mighty kind of you. Honest, mate, we meant you no harm."

"It appears we have a common enemy." I explained about Red and Swift then recounted the story of the crews capture.

"Not surprising. Fast ship he has."

"So, you'll join us then?"

"Sure thing. Michael MacDonald," he said as he extended his hand. "This here's James MacDuggal."

I reached out and shook his hand. "What are two Scotsman doing with the Royal Navy?"

"Pressed into service, we was. Bit of an uprising we had. Damned Brits made short work of putting it down."

That explained their lack of uniform. Taken on as the lowest deckhands, they wouldn't have been given any commission.

"Any skills between you?"

"Happy to kill some Brits."

"Spanish?"

"Them would work as well."

As night closed in and the mosquitoes started to swarm, a fire proved to be a necessity. Blue found a level spot with a flat, stone overhang that would obfuscate the smoke. The small flames did their work keeping the mosquitos at bay. Walking outside of the outcropping we had chosen as a camp I could barely see any sign of our presence, but I had learned my lesson. On returning to camp, I set a watch schedule. Not trusting the newcomers, I set it using only our men.

I gave the freedmen the first watch and lay down on the hard ground, doing my best to make a rock work in place of a pillow. It wasn't the discomfort of my bed, or the pounding in my leg that kept me awake. After a hard day of paddling across the bay and riding overland, my body was exhausted. My growing concern for Shayla, the crew, and our ship—never mind the treasure aboard—kept me awake. The longer we were delayed in reaching Havana and discovering their fate, the more likely we might never find them.

Blue must have felt the same, because before the first dog-watch ended, he was wide awake and pacing. Watching his diminutive figure through the flames, I rose to see what was troubling him.

"We'll get them back," I told him.

"We should go now, Mr. Nick. The moon will be bright enough to travel."

We had already decided that it would take a full day to reach Havana. Leaving now would get us there by noon, allowing the rest of the day to find the crew and ship.

"Right, then. Let's get on with it." I called out to the look-outs above and woke the other men while Juan rigged the horses to the wagon. Within minutes we were assembled and ready to go.

"We'll need to keep a good eye out." I looked at the

shadow cast by the moon. "We should be able to see the road well enough, but no sleeping. Have your weapons ready." I nodded to Blue, who returned the weathered rifle to Michael.

"We should look at that wound of yours before we leave," Blue said.

I didn't want to take the time, but he was right. The pain was to be expected, but it hadn't been properly cleaned. Moving near the remnants of the fire, Blue brought it back to life with a handful of moss and some kindling. Under the growing light, he pulled my leg toward the flames and removed the bandage.

The bleeding had stopped, but the wound was a mess of clotted blood. Tossing the piece of my shirt I'd used as binding into the fire, he cleaned the blood off my leg with a fresh piece of cloth torn from my shirt. While he worked, I tore another strip to use as a bandage.

I breathed deeply, trying to suppress the pain as he worked. The skin was pink from his scrubbing, but a fiery red spot had started to form near the entry hole. There was no need for discussion. We both knew what had to be done, and as I pulled my belt from my pants, Blue heated his knife in the fire.

Placing the bunched-up belt in my mouth, I nodded to the two freedmen at my back. Each man grabbed an arm, and as the blade, heated to a dull red, neared the wound, I could feel their grips tighten. I had suffered this fate once before, and though I knew what to expect it didn't make it any easier. As I screamed into the belt, the men struggled to restrain me while Blue cauterized the entry hole.

The smell of burnt flesh saturated the air as I spit out the belt, and the men relaxed when Blue moved the knife away. Bracing myself for the second round, Blue reheated the knife.

A minute later, sweat covered my face and body as Blue applied a paste made from what he called the Monkey's Hand, a green-leafed vine that grew near the rocks, to my wound, and handed me a piece of bark he had gathered.

"Chew it and suck the juices."

It tasted bitter, but the relief was immediate, though I knew the real pain would come later when the skin around the holes healed. Wrapping the piece of my shirt around the wound, he nodded that he was finished. The freedmen helped me to my feet, and I gingerly tested the leg.

It was a good thing we had the wagon, because my first steps were like those of a sailor after a long voyage. Blue found a branch suitable for use as a staff, and with its help I hobbled across the clearing to the wagon, where Michael and James held the horses by their bridles. Juan was aboard, already in the driver's seat. The freedmen helped me up next to him. I would have preferred to ride in the back, where I could lie down, but if we were seen on the road it wouldn't look right.

Loaded up, Michael and James walked the horses down the narrow path. When we reached the main road, they took their positions. Each with a rifle in hand, James went about a hundred yards ahead, Michael the same distance behind. With our lookouts in place we started down the road toward Havana.

Finding a comfortable position for my leg proved difficult, and when Juan started nodding off, I agreed to take the reins. The moon helped, and since it was well into the dry season all that was required of me was to keep the wheels in the worn tracks. traveling by road in the tropics was generally slow, between the mud and terrain. Ships were often faster, but for now we found ourselves making good time. Though we had no escape from the mosquitos, the night-time temperatures were mild, allowing a respite for the horses.

Dawn found us at a small town. Bringing the Scotsmen in from their positions, we loaded everyone aboard the wagon, stashed the weapons, and hoped for the best. Our precautions were needless, as the only greeting we got through the quiet streets was from a pair of roosters. Blue looked at me. I guessed he wanted to take one, but I shook my head. Several windows were backlit by candles or lanterns, and although we couldn't see the inhabitants, I knew they were watching. We didn't need to stop. We had enough provisions to reach Havana, and if we ran out, we'd hunt our own.

On leaving the town, the road turned east. We'd left the hills behind and found ourselves in a forested land specked with lakes that allowed us to replenish our water supplies. The condition of the road remained good, but it was too narrow for two carts to pass, causing a few delays. With each encounter our hands reached for the concealed weapons, but we got nothing but nods and muted greetings.

Without incident we reached the outskirts of Havana by midday. We'd recently been in the harbor, but I knew little of the city. Everything here happened by the water, and if the crew and ship were being held here, they would likely be held in one of the forts.

As we approached the harbor another concern took hold of me. Our ship, towed by the Spanish frigate, would have been noticed by the watchful eye of the harbormaster. He already had taken our gold in exchange for provisions and weapons, and might have expected there was more treasure aboard. It was well-concealed in the bilge, but a thorough inspection would uncover it. Our only hope was that the bilge would be the last place they looked, giving us a little time.

We blended in well, and so stopped several times to buy food. There were no questions asked as we passed through the city, at least until we were in sight of the harbor and the military presence increased. Still, we were able to travel close enough to see the ships tied to the docks and moored in the harbor. At first, I didn't see her, but once we rounded a corner,

I saw our ship anchored about a hundred yards off the docks. Men were moving aboard, but we were too far away to see if it was our crew or not.

Judging from the two skiffs tied alongside, I guessed that a search was underway.

Chapter 16

STEVEN BECKER

UNCHARTED
Waters

My first inclination was to find a skiff and storm the ship. With only myself and five others, two of whom I didn't completely trust, I thought better of it. Even with greater numbers, attempting to take a ship in the Havana harbor was suicide.

What we needed was information. Roaming the streets as a group would surely attract unwanted attention. Juan and the freedmen had access to areas and information that James, Michael, and I didn't. The converse was true as well. I'd have preferred to stay together, but it was the logical decision to split up. After deciding on a time and meeting place, Juan took the freedmen and headed toward the docks. Much to their delight, the Scots and I found an inn. Blue struck off on his own.

Inside the inn was a hot and sweaty affair, but at least it had shade. Finding a table near the center of the room, the three of us ordered ale and checked our surroundings. Not much of a drinker, I sipped my mug, while James and Michael did what the Scots were known for and quickly downed their first. Blaming the heat of the day and the dusty road for their thirst, they were into their third mugs before I was half-finished with my first. When they order their fourth I had to put a stop to it,

84

reminding them why we were here, and warned them this was their last.

It was hard to focus on any particular conversation in the loud, crowded room. Not surprisingly most were in Spanish, but I was able to pick up on enough words to know they were talking about women, gambling, and ale. There was one group in the corner that caught my attention. They looked as out of place as we did. Michael had turned an ear to them as well.

"That group. Looks like Englishmen to me."

"Surely not Scots from the way they're holding their liquor. Brits never could drink," Michael said.

"Any look familiar?" I asked, watching the group.

Three of the men got up and moved to join a gathering in the corner of the room. Though I couldn't see what they were doing, I had a pretty good idea they were gambling. Rhames would have readily joined the game, but I was as much of a gambler as a drinker. "Either of you good with the dice?"

"We've won our share. Got nothing to wager though," James said, studying the game.

"Right, then. I'll stake you. Just remember, winning is not our goal, information is." I knew as soon as James grabbed the offered coins that my words had fallen on deaf ears. Gold in hand, James was welcomed into the game. Michael followed, watching his partner's back. A minute later they had blended into the group and it looked like my coin was in play.

Watching the game, I strained to see if James had won, but before I could make a determination, a stranger sat down at our table.

"You'd be the captain of that ship in the harbor?"

"And who might be asking?"

"Fair enough. Name's McLean. Justin McLean." He extended a hand, knocking over what little was left in Michael's mug.

"And your business?"

85

He spread his arms wide and knocked over another mug. "Fair enough, Captain."

"Paid for with gold." I inadvertently answered his earlier question. His look changed and I knew he had feigned drunkenness to lower my guard.

"So, it is you."

I cursed myself again, fooled into thinking he was soberer than I. "Right, then." I took his hand. "Nick Van Doren."

"Looks like you've had a run of bad luck, then."

I looked down at my mug and, seeing it nearly empty, drained it and called for two more. A quick glance to the corner confirmed the game was peaceful. Had Rhames been here it might have been a different matter. Having bailed him out of several inequitable—and exciting—affairs, I found myself missing the pirate.

A woman set our fresh mugs down and waited while I fished a few coins from my purse. Realizing I had thrown too much gold around already, I caught several glances from nearby patrons. In response, I laid my rifle on the table to warn any who were more than curious that taking my gold would cost them. With ale flowing freely, though, the weapon might be ignored. I thought it past time to be moving on.

"We've got to go. I'd ask that you plainly state your business."

He drank deeply and set the mug down. "Might have a common interest, you and I."

The game was breaking up, and I felt the need to escape the confines of the inn before word of the money I was spending reached the wrong ears. I rose, beckoning to James and Michael, as well as Justin to follow. The walls seemed to be closing in and every face I passed appeared to have malice in their eyes.

Hobbling on my bum leg, I started for the door, where I was joined by Michael and James. Facing the setting sun, I was temporarily blinded and didn't notice that Justin had not followed, nor did I see the group of men waiting for us outside.

The men were on us before I could see their faces. The first blow had me on my knees, and while trying to rise on my bad leg, a kick to my stomach set me on my back. The pistol flew from my hand, and though I reached for my knife, another hand got to it first. Blows rained down on me and I curled into a fetal position to protect myself, but not before I felt my purse being pulled from my belt.

The gold was gone, but our assailants didn't run. They hovered over me and the two Scots, who were also writhing in pain on the ground. Slowly, I scanned the street. Business, if it ever even had been interrupted, appeared to have resumed as normal. Just as I was about to get my bearings, a boot struck my head, knocking me unconscious.

PAIN SHOT through me when I woke, and slowly, despite my pounding head and swollen eyes, I tried to determine where I was. I could make out the rough iron of the bars in front of me. The cell was small, with a narrow, rectangular slot in the masonry wall that clearly was not big enough for even a child to escape through. Outside it appeared to be night.

Crawling the four feet to the front of the cell, I grabbed the rusted bars. Using them for support I hauled myself to my feet, and looked down the corridor. It was then my head made sense of the noise and smells around me. Cold iron stretched for as far as I could see. Across from me was a badly beaten man. It was surprising that I could recognize him at all through the swelling and bruises, but he was one of the crew.

"Luis?" I whispered across the void, recognizing the freedman from my crew.

"That you, Captain?"

"Quiet now, don't want to advertise that." Now that I had seen him, I pulled my face through the bars and saw several more beaten-up but familiar faces. Taking a chance, I called out for Rhames.

"Couple doors down," the familiar voice came back to me. "Seen ya brought in last night."

I hadn't realized I had been out that long. Leaning against the bars, I ran my hands over my head to check for wounds. My hair matted from what I assumed was dried blood, I found several bumps, but no glaring injuries. My body throbbed with a dull pain from the beating, but the only specific pain was from the gunshot wound to my leg.

"Everyone else here?"

"The men, anyway. Not sure what they've done with the women."

We were in the worst possible situation. With my purse taken and our wealth hidden aboard the ship, now under Spanish custody, my rescue attempt had failed. My prison experience amounted to a few days in Key West, where the men had broken me out. This was a different matter altogether. I knew the Havana jail by reputation—and it wasn't a good one.

While I pondered our options, I studied the cell. About six feet square and made of stone, it had one small window and not much else, although a bucket sat in the corner. I checked it was empty, then carried it to the window. Gripping the uneven stone wall, I pulled myself up. The extra foot or so allowed me to see out, but my view was of only dark water.

Under different circumstances, when we'd sailed through the mouth of the harbor, I had seen the two forts on either side of the entrance. I assumed we were being held in one of them.

Escape was impossible, so I did the only thing I could and yelled for our captors.

Chapter 17

Hobnail-soled boots striking the cement floor signaled the approach of the guard as he leisurely walked down the aisle toward me. From their cells men called out to him as he passed, their greetings generally involving profanity. I was fairly certain it wasn't that the prisoners didn't fear their captors, but that the bars which restrained them also protected them from his wrath.

I continued to yell, so he knew who was calling him, and once he arrived at my cell, I thought I might have acted hastily. He was a giant of a man. Though he'd gone to fat, he still looked immensely strong and his face bore the scars of many battles. It was a seasoned and rare warrior who had more scars than tattoos. Few who were not adept at protecting themselves and taking others' lives survived to become this disfigured.

When he withdrew a large, round key chain and held it close to his face, I had my first clue that he was not invincible. He was clearly myopic—something I hoped to use to my advantage. Finding the key, he inserted it in the lock and with a loud squeal the door opened. He stepped in to find me cowering in the corner.

Kicking the bucket out of the way, he reached down for me. Grabbing the collar of what was left of my shirt, he dragged me like a sack of potatoes out of the cell and down the aisle. Along the walk of shame, I heard catcalls and jokes at my expense and I realized I might have put myself in a worse situation. Near the end of the cellblock stood a pair of steel doors. Withdrawing his keys again, he easily cuffed me with one hand while he opened the door with the other.

Once we were out of the cellblock, I drank in the clean air and looked around at my surroundings. The corridor here was lit by lanterns and I took notice as we passed storerooms, the laundry, and kitchens, all manned by prisoners. Reaching the end of another passage a similar set of gates stopped us. This time the guard called out a name that sounded like "Omar," and a minute later, a man who looked like an Omar came toward us.

They communicated in grunts, and finally Omar opened the door and the guard handed me off to him. Standing several inches taller than the guard, Omar looked like a younger version of him. The lack of a matching belly and scars told me he was both younger and ranked higher than the veteran. In any case, he handled me better than the guard and I soon found myself dropped into the visitor's chair in an office.

I knew the man on the business side of the desk and from the look on his face that probably wasn't a good thing. The last time we'd met, he had sat behind a desk in the harbormaster's office, where we had brokered the deal for our armaments. It appeared he'd taken a fall from grace, and unfortunately it looked like I was to blame.

"Well, look who we have here. The *Capitán* with the treasure."

His accent was thick, but I understood his bitter tone. Hobbling into port after wrecking Lafitte's ships in the Dry

Tortugas, and knowing that Lafitte was their enemy as well, I had used the story of our escape to garner favor with the Spanish. The old saying, "The enemy of my enemy is my friend" rings true—until the sides change.

The Spanish might have had some modest success salvaging Lafitte's ship that had wrecked on the reef. The other ship, which we had taken down with the boom, lay in thirty feet of water—out of their reach. Both ships contained treasure. Apparently, their efforts hadn't been enough and he had been demoted for allowing us to evade him. Now, with my ship and crew under his control, he held all the cards.

"Sir, I ask you what charges are you holding my crew and I on?" The Spanish were sticklers for procedure but, as evidenced in their not-to-distant history, they had no problem burning people alive, either.

"Piracy."

The label we had done our best to lose since Gasparilla's ship was sunk several years ago.

He shuffled some papers, leaned forward, and smiled. "Of course, if you have bills of lading, we would be obliged to review them."

I flinched when his rancid breath hit me. We both knew we had no documentation or provenance for the treasures we had recovered—or for the ship. "There's no ill-gotten gains aboard our ship. Actually, there's not much of anything." I didn't think I'd be sitting here chatting if they'd uncovered the treasure buried in the bilge.

"The search of your ship is ongoing. You and your crew will be brought to justice when the investigation is completed."

I tried to affect a stone face over the combination of smugness and fear I felt. With our conversation at an end, I had to do something, and quickly. The treasure was hidden, but if they were determined to unearth it, the gold would be found.

"The women, what about them? I insist they be treated properly."

He slammed his fist on the desk. "You'll insist nothing."

As I waited for the blood to leave his face an idea occurred to me. "Supposing we cooperate?"

Shaking his hand, he looked up at me. "Don't toy with me, boy."

"Right, then." My mind was racing. "Let's just say there's treasure aboard. Not saying there is, just supposing." Our eyes met, and I had an instant to determine his motives. I'd learned how to read people from Gasparilla, and using what the captain had taught me about the Spanish, I determined it was pride as much as money that fueled the man across the desk. It must have been a blow, not only to his pocketbook but to his social standing, to be demoted to warden of the rat-infested prison. If I could help him get his old position back and line his pockets with some gold while we were at it, I guessed I would have an ally.

"That British officer, the one gone rogue." I was counting on him knowing what had happened with Harp. I saw the recognition in his eyes, but missing was the keen look that would have told me I'd struck gold.

"He's none of our—or your—concern."

"Oh, he most certainly is. Since he and the Brits had their falling-out, he's been attacking your ships. Ask the captain who brought my ship and crew in. You caught us because Harp fled the scene."

"And what of all this?"

I had him off guard now, and took my shot. "There's a small cache aboard the ship in your harbor. I'll hand that over in exchange for the crew and ship."

"We'd find it eventually," he said, dismissing me.

I dropped the sweetener.

"And once we have our ship, I'll lead you to Harp." Now I

had his interest. "We spent some time together when he was anchored right under your noses at the *Isle de los Pinos*. We discussed a rendezvous after our attempted survey of the ship he'd sunk by the reef."

"So, that's what you were up to out there. I've heard tell of your ability to dive."

I had told too much, and if my leg didn't hurt as badly as it did, I would have kicked myself. Lafitte's men must have struck a deal with the Spanish, who rescued them for their freedom. Unfortunately, it was at the crew's and my own expense.

"Our gear was all lost."

His body language told me he knew otherwise. "I'll release you and your crew, but it's treasure, not that British captain, you're going to bring back to me. We know what was lost in the Tortugas." He leaned back in the chair, but before he got comfortable, he rose and walked to the sideboard, where he picked up a crystal decanter and poured a strong inch into a matching glass. Looking at me, he poured another.

He handed me a glass and toasted. "Here's to a prosperous partnership." A smile crossed his face before he drank.

I raised my glass and drained it, not to signify that we had a deal, but hoping the alcohol would temper the pain of my leg. Tossing me an approving look, he finished his drink, took a rolled-up chart from a bin behind him, and motioned me to a work table full of books.

He started to sweep the books off the table, but I intervened, not wanting to see them damaged. Several armfuls later, the books were neatly stacked in the corner and the chart was laid out on the table.

"Show me where you ran that clever little boom of yours." He handed me a keel.

I had no reason to disguise the locations. He already knew the area, and we had no intentions of going back—at least on our own. Taking the marker, I placed a light circle around the area.

"And where the ships lie."

Recalling the scene, I drew several small circles with asterisks inside. "Here's the reef we sent the ship you've already salvaged." I drew the outline of a small boat, its bow buried in the coral symbols. "But you already know that."

"We got little off her. The survivors' recollection is that she sank stern first. The bulk of what she carried is on the bottom."

That explained his abrupt fall from grace. It was time to make a deal.

Chapter 18

An hour later, the crew, minus Shayla and Lucy, were reunited. The windowless room lacked bars, but the guard outside our door reminded us that we were still behind the last set of gates beyond which freedom lay. My confirmation of the deception that had led to the wrecks, and our subsequent escape from Lafitte's ships, had the warden optimistic about our efforts, but he had insisted the women remain behind as his "guests." I made it clear our agreement was void unless Blue and I saw them before our departure.

The men were in good spirits—freedom had that effect on people. The two Scots fit in well. Though they would not take Swift's and Red's places, they gravitated toward Rhames. Juan and Beauchamp were noticeably absent, but I could get no information on his whereabouts. There was little trust for the warden, but at least our confinement was over. The arrangement would be much the same as our salvage of the *Panther*, except our share was our freedom, and hopefully, if he kept his word, our ship and women.

I had insisted that our ship being held hostage in the harbor be given back to our control. Instead of sending escorts, which I guessed the warden no longer had the authority to do, we were to sail with a contingent of Spanish naval men aboard, one with the rank of captain who would be in charge of the ship. For a man currently without authority the arrangement made sense. The ship leaving the harbor would be noticed, but the story was that it was being sent to Mantanzas to pick up a load of sugar. When it returned with gold instead, the warden hoped to be elevated back to his previous position.

The guard who had led me to the warden earlier called from the door. I motioned for Blue and we followed him down the corridor to another, smaller room. Once inside, we ran to our women, but with the guard looking on, we kept our greetings platonic.

"Are you alright?" I asked Shayla.

"Yes," she said, looking me up and down. "I should be asking that question of you. What happened?"

I wasn't sure how much time we would be allowed, and motioning for Blue and Lucy to come closer, I gave a summary of our situation.

"Seems we're just tools in a bigger game," Shayla said, as she caressed the bruises on my face.

This was not a discussion I wanted to get into now.

"Mr. Nick. What happened to your leg?" Lucy asked, kneeling to look at my wound.

"Should be alright now. We cauterized it."

"If I had my bag, I could make you a poultice," she said loud enough for the guard to hear.

Both women started to investigate my injuries.

Shayla turned to the guard. "He needs attention. Get their bags."

The man only grunted. From what I had observed, my condition was about average for the inmates here. The guard started toward us, signifying that the liaison was over.

"We'll be back for you—I swear it," were the last words I

said before Blue and I were pulled from the room. The door slammed and I heard Shayla's voice, I hoped not for the last time. The guard led us back to the larger room, where the men were enjoying a meal. From their appearance and the way they gorged themselves on the food, it appeared they hadn't been fed until now. With the sight and scent of the chicken and pork laid out on the table, my stomach grumbled, and I realized I was starved as well. Heading for the food, I took a plate. Looking around the room to ensure the men had gotten their fill, I loaded it high and took it to the corner where Rhames was sitting.

"I could thank you for coming after us, but next time, it'd be better not to get caught yourself. And the women?"

"We've just seen them. The warden intends to hold them until we return."

"Then we should be getting on with it."

I was grateful for his good attitude, but knew he was anxious to go after Harp. I assured him that Red and Swift were on my mind as well. "They're to shuttle us out in the morning after the ship's been provisioned. I don't expect to have much time aboard before we weigh anchor."

After finishing my supper, I sought out Mason and we gathered the men together. Under guard, there was no talk of deception or escape. I explained the deal with the warden, and answered any questions I could. With the only other option being prison, there was no need for a vote to ratify.

We were allowed to stay in the room overnight. Soon before dawn, we were fed again, and as the first light of freedom showed through the narrow windows, chained together like slaves the jailers led us to a waiting skiff. Growing up Dutch, I was never in favor of slavery, and never experienced the tragedy of one man owning another firsthand. Our restraints made it awkward to load the skiff, and I couldn't help but notice that between our crew and the weight of our restraints the freeboard was only inches above the water. "Helpless" was the word that came to mind, and I felt the pain of the men and women of color who had made this trip before me.

Fortunately, the harbor was still, and we reached the ship without incident, for the weight of any water that might have made its way aboard would have sunk us. Had we swamped, with our hands and feet in chains, we would sink directly to the bottom, joining uncounted others.

The sun was low, sending a glare over the water that would prevent any onlookers from seeing us as we were rushed into the forward hold. Having only a skeleton crew ourselves, we had rigged the ship to be sailed by a handful of men, and it appeared we weren't needed. Voices called back and forth in Spanish. I didn't understand much of it, but the activity on deck was familiar to a ship leaving port, and I soon heard the chain rattle around the capstan as the anchor was hauled aboard.

Several hot hours later a man appeared in the hatch. "Which one of you's the captain and the navigator?"

His English was broken but adequate, which would prove to be good and bad. We could communicate without needing Shayla to translate, but he could also understand us. We'd have to be careful with any talk of taking the ship.

"You can take the chains off now," I said.

"And, you must be the captain." The man spat on the deck.

"Right, then. Mason here is the navigator." There was no reason, at least at this point, not to be cooperative.

With our shackles removed, Mason and I were brought on deck. "Captain. My name is Van Doren. This is Mason."

"I'd be the first mate, then. The captain is indisposed," he said, leading us to the helm. Laid out on the binnacle was our map of the Tortugas. "I'd warn you beforehand. With your men in chains, there'll be no deception. This ship goes down, they'll go with it."

I understood the threat.

"The notations are accurate," Mason said, leaning over the chart. "If it were me, I'd come in from this side. The reef closes in there." He pointed to the annotations he had made on the chart.

The look on the first mate's face told me that he didn't like the proposed detour. "We've got as much at stake in this as you, sir. There's no reason not to trust us."

"I've heard the stories, Van Doren. A quick study you are."

"Again, our aim is the same. The warden is holding our women until we return."

"Never seen a pirate loyal to his woman," he snorted.

I wasn't about to engage him in a discussion on pirates. The best thing we could do was to be agreeable. An opportunity would present itself—one generally did, and if not we'd make one.

"You and your men can earn some measure of freedom aboard, but I'll tell you right now, it won't be much."

Fearing that our conversation was at an end, I glanced around the deck, studying the Spanish crew. If Rhames were with us, he would have already taken measure of our opponent. Without his eyes, and with Mason more concerned about how the crew had trimmed the sails, I took in every detail I could.

As I expected we were dismissed, but before we were taken back to the hold I turned to the mate. "We'll need some time with the gear before we dive. Tides'll play a factor in the recovery as well."

"Looked adequate to me, and you'll dive when I tell you to dive. Back to the hold for you." He nodded to the men standing behind us, who escorted us back below.

Chapter 19

From the sound of the water rushing underneath the hull and the attitude of the ship, I had a general idea that we would arrive on site by nightfall. Under other circumstances I would have let the captain and navigator seek their own council, but with the crew and myself in chains, striking the reef would likely lead us to our deaths.

Calling up to the deck, I asked to speak to the first mate. A few minutes later, I was dragged up the ladder and brought to the helm.

"Something I can help you with, Van Doren?" He blew a puff of smoke from his pipe and watched as the wind took it. "Fair weather. Seems we've had a bit of luck crossing the straits."

The Straits of Florida can be a treacherous, but not nearly as dangerous as the shoals scattered through the Tortugas. "Just wondering if you've been in these waters?"

"Suppose you'd like a look at my twenty years of log books?"

He'd been a first mate almost as long as I'd been alive,

leaving me to wonder why he hadn't been promoted to captain. "No sir, not questioning your ability."

"What's your point, then?"

"Just that there're more reefs than those marked on the chart. A lot more, actually. I'd suggest you heave-to overnight and approach in the morning."

He pulled hard enough on his pipe that I could see the embers in the bowl glow, and took his time before he exhaled, blowing the smoke in my face. "And when I'll be wanting your opinion, I'll ask for it. Only a fool would sail into that death trap at night."

"Right, then. Sorry to have bothered you."

He waved his hand. "Never mind. I suppose since you're on deck already, you might have a look at your gear. Don't have enough of you to lose anyone down there."

I was glad for the opportunity to be out of the hold. "I could use my man Rhames."

"One man." He turned to the crewman who had brought me up from the hold and asked him to retrieve Rhames.

Before I could thank him, he turned and, with a puff of smoke lingering on the breeze, was gone. While I waited for Rhames, I scanned the water for any indication of our position. Though it meant little, it was habit. All around us was the deep, dark, indigo water of the straits. Ahead, and low on the horizon, I could see several puffy clouds, suggesting the proximity of the larger islands in the area.

"Captain?" Rhames greeted me after he was unfettered.

"Right, then," I said. "Let's go through the gear." I winked at him and saw his sly smile.

"Whatever you'd be needing."

Boredom is the enemy of any guard, and it was my goal to lull the two men nearby into that state. Slowly and thoroughly I ran my hands along the hoses, examining them for any nicks or tears. I took note of several abrasions that caught my eye. In the end, I found no repairs were necessary, though a fresh coating of lard would help preserve the hoses.

"There're divers below, more suited for this work," Rhames said.

He was as bored as the guards. "Have a look around: men, armaments, anything that might help later," I whispered.

"I got your meaning, Captain. What say we stretch these baby's down the length of the deck?"

"Right, then." I started to walk with the hose, and winced in pain.

"Leg still bothering you then?" Rhames asked.

"I'll be alright." I grit my teeth and continued.

I asked one of the men charged with watching us for a tub of lard to grease the hoses.

When he returned, we took both hoses and extended them to their limits. Coating them with the lard as we laid them out, we were able to check out the ship.

"Got a good idea what we're up against," Rhames whispered. "Might want to hang onto that tub of lard. Got some idea it might come in handy."

Coiling the hoses, we stowed them and checked the face mask. After just the single dive, it appeared to be in good condition. Trying to focus on the coming effort, I thought back to what improvements were needed. The experiment had been brief, but I did remember the fog on the glass causing problems.

Placing the sailcloth-clad bucket on my head, I waited for the glass to fog. It took less time than I expected. Removing the helmet, I spat on my hand, then inserted it in the opening and rubbed it on the glass. The fog disappeared quickly. Placing the helmet back on my head, I waited. After a few minutes, sweat started to drip from my brow, but the glass remained clear.

Hoping I had solved the problem, I removed the helmet. Before I could set it down, the deck dropped out from beneath my feet.

My first thought was that we had struck something, but as I started to rise, I felt my head start to spin, and lay back down.

"Get Blue," I called to Rhames.

I was in the shade when I came to, and it took me a minute to remember what had happened. Rhames was among the group surrounding me. Before I could focus on the rest of the faces, a sharp pain came from my leg.

"Blast, it's gotten infected," a bespectacled man said.

From his age and build, I guessed he was the carpenter or cook. It was common for either or both to share the duties of a doctor aboard.

"Get Blue." All I could do was mutter though my clenched jaw as the man lanced the wound.

The group jumped back to avoid the puss that flew from the abscess.

"Blue, one of my men. He'll know what to do."

"Best deal with it quickly or that leg needs to come off."

I was so focused on the thought of losing my leg that I didn't notice the "doctor" send one of the men to bring Blue. From the look on his face, he didn't want to take the leg off any more than I wanted him to. My confirmation came when he removed a flask from his pocket, drank deeply, and handed it to me.

The liquor steeled me enough to look down at the wound. Red lines shot from the site the bullet had entered up and down my leg. Just as I saw the extent of it, Blue appeared.

The group stepped back, allowing him access to me. It didn't take long for his evaluation. "We need to find the fish weed."

Everyone looked at him, never having heard of fish weed.

Were it not for the pounding in my head I might have figured it out, but I was preoccupied with pain and fear.

"The fish weed, Mr. Nick."

It was Rhames that solved the riddle. "The weeds where the little bugger catches the dorado."

Having seen Blue and Lucy fish, I knew what he was talking about now. It was the sargassum that floated in lines or large rafts, depending on the current. Whenever we spotted the weeds, we altered course when we could to allow Blue and Lucy to troll their baits underneath or nearby. Nine times out of ten they caught fish.

I described the weed to the doctor and he called for several of the men to climb the rigging and search out some.

"How much time do we have?" I asked, knowing that in the fading light, the odds of spotting some of the weed was small.

When he didn't answer, the looks turned solemn and the flask was handed back to me. Hoping for any relief, I drank deeply. Thankfully, one of the lookouts saw something and called down to the deck. Were it not for the moon, I doubted he would have seen the patch. During the day there are the birds that generally fly over the patches waiting for an errant baitfish to venture outside the protective perimeter. At night they were near invisible.

The ship turned hard in the direction the lookout had pointed. The men gathered around the rail, ready with long hooks, used for backing sails and boarding other ships, which they used to pluck the seaweed from the water. Blue grabbed an armful of the seaweed and brought it to me.

"This should help," he said, starting to cover my leg in the wet, cool seaweed. Whether it was working or not didn't matter in the moment—it helped with the pain.

"Leave it on until it dries out." Blue walked toward a bucket with a rope attached, used to haul up seawater for cleaning and such. Holding the end of the line, he tossed the bucket into the sea. Hand over hand, he retrieved it and when it was over the rail, he dropped the rest of the seaweed in the water.

I spent the next few hours keeping the weed wet and wondering how I would fare with one leg.

Chapter 20

Wishing for a breeze to evaporate the sweat pouring from my body, darkness finally fell bringing some relief from the heat. The dangers of a becalmed ship hadn't occurred to me until just after the second dog watch. My earlier worries about striking one of the dangerous shoals during the night was replaced by the fear that we would drift into the Gulf Stream's strong current. Without wind in our sails to counteract the six-knot river running through the Atlantic, we would be driven far off course, not a situation I relished with my men in chains.

Mason took over, appearing at my side and giving me his report of sorts. It was difficult for both of us. Despite my injuries I was his captain, and he was the best navigator I knew. Watching others do our jobs aboard our own ship was difficult. Blue continued to fuss with the seaweed, reassuring me that it would work even as he was escorted below.

"Mr. Nick. If I had my bag …" His voice disappeared as he was dragged into the hold with the rest of the crew.

"What'd he say?" I asked Mason.

"Something about his satchel. Maybe he's got some medicine."

In my current state I was willing to try anything short of the sawbones cure. "I'd like to speak to the captain," I called to one of the guards.

"Wouldn't we all," he replied.

The captain had been invisible since we had boarded. I knew many officers liked to spend their time in their cabins, but I preferred to mingle with the crew and take my share of the watches.

"If he wants a chance of some gold tomorrow, he'll listen," I told the guard.

That got him to thinking, probably more about the reprisals he might face by disregarding my request than his concern about whether we dove or not. Things were different aboard a naval vessel than a pirate ship, and there was a good chance the men didn't know about our mission—or the gold. I'd always been forthright with my crew, knowing that men live by rumors aboard a ship. I'd rather my crew had the truth.

His decision made, he got up and went toward the companionway. A few minutes later he returned with the captain. I wasn't sure what I expected from a Spanish officer at sea, but the disheveled man in a robe who looked the worse for drink was not it. I was more worried about disturbing him than about the liquor on his breath. I'd spent the last dozen years dealing with drunks, that I could handle. An angry captain with complete authority over me was another story.

"Thank you, Captain," I said. Gritting my teeth against the pain, I scooted myself up to a sitting position.

"You're looking the worse for wear," he replied, slurring his words.

"The wound's festered and I'm running a fever. My man, the African Pygmy, has some medicine in his bag. It was brought aboard with us."

He immediately ordered one of the guards to find the bag. He mumbled, but his voice was loud, and I was able to understand enough words that I sensed he wanted me kept alive—at all costs.

The bag appeared and the captain asked that Blue be brought from the hold. Blue might have been distressed by my condition, but seeing his bag brought a smile to his face—until one of the guards dumped its contents on the deck.

The darts for the blowgun were confiscated, as was a knife. Everything else seemed innocuous enough, and he motioned Blue towards the pile of his belongings. I had seen Lucy mutter words that sounded like a curse before, and what Blue was saying under his breath could be nothing else.

"Here," he said, placing a piece of the bark he had collected the other night between my teeth.

While I worked the tree bark, pulling what liquid I could, he gathered up his belongings and started to sort through them. After replacing them in his bag, he returned to my side and removed the seaweed from my leg. The wound looked different, not as angry as earlier, and slowly I noticed the pain had subsided as well. Thanking Blue while he replaced the old weed with fresh sargassum from the bucket, I started to take notice of my surroundings.

"I need to speak to Rhames," I whispered to Blue.

"I'll get the bastard for you."

His imitation of the pirate brought a smile to my face. "You do that," I said, and reaching for his arm I brought him close to my face. "Spread the word that I'm working on a plan."

When he smiled his teeth gleamed in the moonlight. By all signs his cure was working. Despite his diminutive size the Spaniards treated him with a guarded respect that I suspected was fueled by superstition. I had seen Blue and Lucy's "magic" and understood its roots, though I would never reveal their secrets.

Blue left, and Rhames appeared a few minutes later.

"Lookin' a bit better then, Captain." The old pirate fingered the leather thong around his neck that held the key to the armory.

At first, I thought this might be the break we needed, but then realized that without the key our captors would have broken the lock and replaced it with one of their own. The old key was nothing more than a talisman now.

"Right, then." I moved to stand.

"Sure you're up to it?" Rhames asked, grabbing my arm as I got to my feet.

"We need to talk, and I need to see if this leg still works." Using his shoulder for support, I added weight to the wounded leg. Surprisingly it held, and I continued to test it until my weight was balanced almost normally. I felt sturdy, but weak.

"Give me a hand and we'll see what the foredeck has to offer."

The guards watched as we walked toward the bow. With one arm around Rhames and the other clutching the rail, I moved forward. Watching an injured man on the deck of a ship is light duty, and the guards seemed happy to stay where they were as long as we remained in sight.

"Any ideas?" I asked Rhames when we were out of earshot.

"Not unless we can get the key to the hold and unlock the men. We've got equal numbers, but the chains are a disadvantage."

"I've an idea." I explained my thoughts to him. "I can't dive, though. You'll have to explain what we need."

"Aye, I'll tell the boys, then it'd be up to them," he replied.

I felt surprisingly good as we walked back to the hatch cover that had been converted to my temporary bed. Adding some yelps of pain and various moans and groans for the benefit of the guards, I lay back down. The spot was perfect for observing the comings and goings of the ship, and was within earshot of the binnacle. I feigned pain, hoping I wouldn't be returned to the hold.

Blue, Mason, and Rhames took turns through the night to be by my side, and on each visit, we walked back to the foredeck where I could explain my plan. Adding their input, by morning we had something that might work, but it relied on the wreck that we had yet to find.

As suddenly as it had departed with the night, the wind returned in the morning, bringing clear skies with it. I listened intently as the helmsman gave his report to the captain. It took a minute to translate the numbers for our longitude and latitude from Spanish to English, but once I had them, I plotted our location in my head. If the wind held, I expected we would be on site in a few hours.

Concluding his business at the helm, I was the first mate's next stop.

"We'll be nearing the site soon."

"Right, then. Have you ever found a wreck before?" I asked.

"Not from the depths."

That put me in a better position. "There should be an extra hundred feet of anchor rode aboard."

"What would you have me do with it?"

"It's a simple enough matter. Anchor close to my man's mark. Then send two skiffs to drag the chain between them. When it snags on something, one of the divers will investigate. It'll be a tedious process with all the reefs running through the area, but we'll find it."

He thought for a second and nodded his head at the simple plan. I had no problem helping him find the wreck and even diving on it, for while we recovered the riches from the ocean floor, we'd be stockpiling the weapons for our escape.

Chapter 21

The sound of the bell woke me from a fitful sleep. I heard my name being called and sat up, only to find myself covered in sweat. My leg continued to pound, but it was a different kind of pain, more dull than sharp, and one I had experienced before. Still, after seeing the red lines emanating from the wound last night, I was hesitant to peek under the weeds.

The swelling had subsided, and I leaned forward to remove the dried seaweed. The redness had receded to a small area, making me hopeful I would be keeping my appendage. Blue arrived a minute later to confirm my opinion.

"Help me up?" I asked.

Last night in my weakness, my weight would have pulled him back towards me, but my strength had returned enough that I needed little assistance to rise. Testing the leg again, I was relieved, and though it was painful, I was able to walk unassisted.

"Have you got any more of that magic tree bark?" I asked, as I heard my name called from the binnacle

He reached into his bag and handed me a piece.

Placing it in my mouth and chewing like it was a piece of

dried fish, I hobbled to the binnacle. The first mate and navigator were huddled over the chart. "If you bring Mason up, he'll guide you through."

I could tell both men were torn between taking their chances with the coral structures lurking only a few feet below the keel, and turning over control of the ship to a prisoner. After a quick discussion, one of the men was dispatched to get Mason.

"I'll need the divers as well. It takes some time to prepare."

"Let's find the bloody thing first," the mate said.

There was no reason to push him now and I relented. Mason appeared with the man and walked toward the binnacle as if it were his—which it was.

I moved closer and watched as he dragged a finger across the worn paper, tracing a line that would be the best approach. The navigator handed him a pencil, but he refused, instead stepping to the wheel. The man on duty looked back at the first mate, who nodded his consent. The look of satisfaction on Mason's face as he took command of the ship was priceless, and in that moment, I renewed my vow to find Harp and take the schooner. That coming right after we escaped from this predicament, made it back to Havana to rescue Lucy and Shayla, and had our oft-postponed wedding.

"From the masthead your lookouts should be able to see the two outcroppings. Anchoring will depend on the current, but we'll want the stern in the gap between them." I had a picture in my head of the area just past the *Tongue*. It would be difficult to leave behind the gold-filled diving bell we had used to anchor the boom that had taken out Lafitte's ships, but if the Spanish didn't know it was there, I had no intention of telling them.

With the aid of the lookouts, Mason wound the ship past the *Tongue* and called for the anchor. The chain rattled as the hook fell the thirty feet to the bottom, and we waited until the ship settled back, ending up about a dozen feet from where I had expected to find the wreck.

"We'll need to deploy the skiffs. Your choice if we drag a chain or just dive."

The first mate considered this for a minute. "If you're confident of the location, let's get the divers in the water. See how good you really are."

"I'll manage them from here. This leg's going to keep me above the surface."

He snorted in disgust.

"The men are trained and know what to do." I explained the shifts that had worked for us in Cozumel to prevent the diving sickness.

"You'll have your way with it, but results had better be forthcoming—and quickly," he said. Walking toward the bow he entered the companionway. I expected he would be giving the captain a full report.

Because of my injury I now had freedom aboard. Hoping that between Rhames, Mason, and Blue the word had gotten out that I had a plan, I walked, or rather stumbled, into the hold. Greetings came from the men, and looking from face to face, although they were in chains their spirits were high. They'd had water, and been fed. Hopefully the word that we had a plan had circulated.

"Right, then. Shouldn't be long now, men. We're above the wreck. In an hour we'll start diving and see if we can't bring up some treasure."

"You mean to split it with these bastards?" Rhames piped up.

I had seen him wink at the crew, and then me, before his bit of stagecraft. The captain would be a fool to have no spies and Rhames was a master at misinformation.

"We want our freedom?" I called to the crew.

The men nodded in agreement.

"We'll have to trust them for the time being. Our focus, unless we want another, longer, stay in the Havana jail is to recover as much treasure as we can."

They muttered in agreement. For my plan to be successful, we needed to cooperate with our captors—until we were ready. "Divers, I need you on deck. The rest of you will work in the skiffs supporting them."

They understood that this meant they were at least going to get out of the hold. I called up to the guard, asking him to release the divers. As they reached the deck, the six men I had trained in Cozumel squinted from the sun as their eyes adjusted to the daylight. When they had acclimated, I reviewed my plan and picked the team leaders.

We'd come a long way in our underwater endeavors. A good deal depended on training and experience, but it turned out there was also some science to the business. Diving came with a variety of mild maladies: nausea, headaches, aching joints, and loss of feeling in their limbs. These less-severe symptoms usually cleared in a day or so if the man was kept out of the water. More acute symptoms could result in permanent injury or death.

I'd come upon a rotation of sorts, mostly due to our equipment limitations. Working the men in teams allowed for rest periods between their efforts. As incentive to the men, I kept a ledger to track their dives, which increased their share. In the process, though it had taken some time, I noticed a pattern. The more rest the divers got, the less likely they were to suffer from the sickness.

Taking the team leaders aside, we found a quiet spot by the rail, where I reviewed our plan. They had all worked with the equipment, and I told them about my discovery that spitting on the glass might help keep it from fogging. After the schedule was sorted, I brought them closer.

"We need treasure to keep the Spanish happy, but more

than that, we need to stockpile whatever weapons you can. First though, we need to salvage small pieces of metal to use to pick the locks on our restraints. Have the men hide those in their clothing and we'll try them tonight. Everything else stays in piles by the wreck. But remember, we need enough gold to keep the Spanish happy."

They nodded their understanding and each man returned to his team. While the first group brought the equipment to the stern, I found the guard and had the other men brought on deck. Rhames and Mason led the half-dozen freedmen who would be responsible for the pumps and hoses feeding air to the diver. They would also handle the lines and rigging of the block and tackle, should anything of value be discovered.

We were all ready, but first we needed to find the wreck. Anchored over the *Tongue*, I would have liked to climb the rigging for a better look at the bottom, but didn't trust my leg. In my place, I sent Blue. He returned a few minutes later and described the formations guarding the narrow channel.

If we had been searching on a clear piece of sandy bottom, using the skiffs and dragging a chain between them might have been the answer, but in this maze of coral I feared the chain would constantly snag. We were close enough to the reef, and I had a good idea where the ship had gone down, making diving the better alternative.

The skiffs were made ready. Our teams consisted of three divers each. One would use the headgear, and the other two would free dive in support. The first man was ready, and I watched from the stern rail of the ship. He slid into the water, followed by the freedivers. There was nothing I could do except wait.

Chapter 22

Each team had dived twice without success. Unable to do anything besides watch, I became restless as the divers worked. It felt better to walk than sit, and I paced the deck.

"How's the leg holding up?" Mason asked as I passed the binnacle.

He was hunched over the old chart, talking to the Spanish navigator. Moving toward them, I grew curious as to how they were communicating. Mason had no Spanish, and I didn't think the navigator had English. There is a common bond between men in their position who often cross lines to share information that could save them in the hopes another navigator might someday return the favor. Standing right behind them, I could see they were using the symbols, standard to charts regardless of their origin, to communicate. It looked like Mason was showing the navigator the approaches to our location. As he drew in the hazards we had encountered on our previous trip, I had an idea.

"Can you draw the route Lafitte's ship took? From where they closed the gap to her striking the boom." I turned to the navigator. "If I can have a look at the logbook, I can see what the state of the tide was when she wrecked." He seemed to understand what I was after and the help it might be in finding the treasure. Holding up a finger, he signaled he would be right back and disappeared into the companionway.

"What are you up to?" Mason asked.

"If we can plot the ship's course prior to striking the boom, then apply the tides and currents recorded in the log to her bearing, we might be able to pinpoint her location. The divers have each had two attempts. They've seen nothing but coral."

"Aye," he said, folding the chart over. Taking a pencil, he drew the underwater landmarks we knew: *The Tongue* and the coral formations lining the channel where we had led Lafitte's ships.

He stopped and closed his eyes, as if he was trying to remember the details. "Right here is where we dropped the bell." He made a small "X" on the map. "Then we moved off to about here." Another "X" marked the ship's location. He drew a dotted line between them to illustrate the chain. Looking back, then forward, he tried to recall the course Lafitte's ship had taken.

I took the pencil and drew a faint line from memory. Mason had been looking forward, intent on getting our ship through the narrow channel. I had been the one checking on Lafitte's ships as they followed us into the trap.

"Could be about right," he said.

Just as we had plotted the course, the navigator appeared carrying the logbook. Setting it on the binnacle, I opened it to the last page and scanned backwards until I reached the fateful day. Now we needed to apply the tide and currents that had been recorded in Mason's hand. In retrospect, we were lucky it had been low tide; had it been high, our ruse might have failed. Mason's notations were clear: low tide and an easterly current of about two knots.

"Current would have pushed her hard toward the reef," I

said, trying to picture what the conditions would do to a ship on the way to her grave.

"Considering the water's only thirty feet, maybe got a hundred feet or so of push."

Looking back over the rail at the location of the skiffs, they were at least a hundred feet off the mark. With Mason in tow, I limped to the stern and directed them to where we suspected the wreck lay. Now that we had a better idea of the ship's resting place, I wished that I could be the one diving on her, or at least aboard the skiff, where I could get firsthand information.

Mason and I were fairly certain the men were diving on the right spot now, but the hours ticked by and the divers changed crews twice more before one of the men yelled back to the ship that they had found something. That could still mean nothing. A wreck didn't usually cooperate and drop intact to the sea bottom—especially after her bottom was torn out by a chain boom. The wreck and her contents could be scattered across a large expanse of bottom. The only thing in our favor was that it was recent. At least there had been no major storms to further dismember her since she sank.

The first skiff was anchored on top of the divers and, not wanting to interrupt their operations, I called the other boat over. While they rowed toward the rope ladder hanging from the stern, I tested my wounded leg by increasing the weight I placed on it, finding that though it was painful, standing on it was bearable. If I could do that, there was no reason I couldn't climb down the ladder and get closer to the action.

Adding in the sway of the ship and the awkward nature of the ladder, it was harder than I expected, especially the last few feet. Waiting on the lowest rung for the movement of the ladder and the skiff to coincide, I finally dropped to the deck. Pain shot through my leg, but I ignored it as the men rowed us toward the newer boat the Spanish had provided to replace our burnt one.

There was a general air of excitement aboard the skiff. After testing my leg on the rope ladder, I felt there would be no harm in checking the wreck myself. Seeing it firsthand, if only for a minute, would allow me to direct the salvage operation.

"I'm going to have a look," I called across to the skiff with the divers aboard.

"Diver should be up in another minute. It was the freediver that reported on the sighting."

With the skiffs rafted together, I carefully climbed over the gunwales and, careful to stay out of the hoses and lines, took the middle seat on the diver's skiff. Resisting the urge to lean toward starboard, where a flurry of bubbles broke the surface, so as not to tip the skiff, I watched as the diver's head, or rather the headgear, broke the surface.

As soon as the helmet was lifted off the diver's head the questions started. I sat back and listened, knowing soon enough, I would see it firsthand.

"Right, then. While we've still got some daylight." The men readied the equipment for me.

Minutes later, I spat on my hands, rubbed the saliva on the face mask, and slid into the water. Hanging onto the side of the skiff, the men placed the heavy lead-weighted helmet over my head and gave me the signal that all was ready. A second later fresh air started to pour into the chamber and I released my grip and dropped into the water. Two men accompanied me to the bottom, then kicked back to the surface to renew their air supply.

Even before the silt caused by my landing had cleared, I could see the stern of the ship. She lay just as Mason and I had plotted her, though it was clear the hull had been split by the boom. Walking toward the ship, I was surprised to feel no pain in my leg. I knew the pressures at depth differed than those on the surface. As we had observed, the helmet was awkward and heavy above, but needed to be weighted underwater. The same applied to my body, which benefited from the increased buoyancy.

In the few minutes I had been down, it had started to darken and I suspected the sun was just about to set. Taking bigger strides, I made it to within a few feet of the hull before the hose drew tight. There was no time to surface and reset the skiff. I briefly thought about removing the gear and swimming around the wreck. It took two men to remove the helmet at the surface. I knew I could free myself, but worried about putting it back on. Taking in as many details as I could, I studied the ship.

I was so engrossed in my observations that I flinched when a shadow crossed in front of me. My first thought was that it was a shark, but it turned out to be one of the freedivers sent to recall me to the surface. I gave him the thumbs-up signal and lifted my arms to allow him to place a line around me. Once it was set, he tugged twice, and I braced myself for the ascent.

Breaking the surface, I waited patiently while the men removed the gear and helped me climb aboard. Once I was sorted out, I answered the question on everyone's lips.

"She's there alright, and more or less intact."

Chapter 23

The captain made a brief appearance on deck when we returned to the ship. After seeing his condition last night I hadn't expected to see him at all. He appeared to be in pain, and I couldn't help but notice a limp as he walked. A smile broke through his grimace and I could tell by his expression that he had heard of our success. With the wreck ensconced in thirty feet of water, I felt secure in our position and was not concerned about showing a little emotion. We were now a necessity. I had heard rumors about others experimenting with dive gear, but these stories mostly came from across the Atlantic. To my knowledge, there was no one else in the Caribbean capable of an efficient salvage effort at depth.

Exhausted from even my limited efforts, but well enough that the captain judged me fit to be put back in the hold, I tried to get comfortable. After two nights aboard, each man had developed his own position for sleeping within the limits of their shackles. After only a few hours it made me wonder how another human could survive the journey from Africa to the Americas.

I finally fell into a restless sleep, only to be awakened by the man next to me trying to get comfortable. As I lay awake in the hold, I pictured Shayla in my mind, vowing somehow, we would get back to Havana and rescue her. After a time, the image of the wreck replaced her and I eased myself into a sitting position while I made a mental plan of how to attack the wreck.

As cumbersome and dangerous as it was to work underwater, it was crucial to salvage the wreck as efficiently as possible. We'd done this on several wrecks over the last few years, including our own *Panther*. Each had their own peculiarities. Some stood erect, as if they had just stopped and sunk. Others were scattered over large expanses of the ocean floor.

Lafitte's ship was not intact, but neither was it totally demolished. From my quick survey, the ship had split in two. I'd never been aboard, but the design of the ship was similar to many I had been on. If it was consistent with the other boats of its style, we should be able to easily locate the holds.

Unless one of my own crew was a spy, the captain had no way of knowing what we were up to down there. I had to assume my men were loyal, but it didn't matter. We needed to produce something for our efforts to meet the terms of the agreement I had made with the warden back in Havana. With one set of gear it would be difficult to do any exploration outside our given task—to bring up gold.

Finally, my mind shut down and I fell asleep.

THE MORNING BROUGHT A GENTLE SWELL, probably generated by a far-off storm. Locally though, the conditions were good. A light breeze cooled the sweat on our bodies and the lazy, puffy clouds brought intermittent but welcome relief from the sun. Before the first team hit the water we developed a plan. Assuming that the wreck hadn't caved in on itself as it struck the bottom, the treasure should still be in one of the holds.

The diver for the first team would enter the wreck from the gash amidships and search toward the stern. I had asked for some paper to diagram the ship, and to my surprise had my logbook returned. Before we boarded the skiffs, I made a sketch, drawing the wreck as I remembered it, and placed arrows at what I hoped to be clear points of entry.

The first diver would penetrate the wreck from the starboard side; the second diver, the port side. I could only hope there was enough space and light available. The option was to dismember the ship from the top, a long and exhausting process. While the diver with the headgear worked, one of the freedivers was assigned to stay with him while the other was tasked with collecting metal scraps that might work to pick the locks on our restraints.

Any dive that everyone returns from is a good dive. And that was the only satisfaction we got as we worked through the morning. I could tell without having to look over at the ship that we were being watched—and our captors were probably not happy with the divers returning empty-handed. With each diver having been down twice, I called the noon-time break, which was generally a couple of hours, something that helped to fight off the diving sickness.

Leaving the skiff's anchor attached to a buoy, we returned to the ship hoping to get out of the sun for a few hours. Moving past the grim expressions of the Spanish, I wasn't sure what they had been expecting, but from the looks on their faces, it had probably been gold. Their expressions told me that their patience was already wearing thin.

Seeking out the captain to give him an update, I was told

he was unavailable, and that the first mate would see me. I explained that we had found the wreck, but were having trouble getting to the hold. His attitude was less forgiving than the captain's had been, and he dismissed me with a not-so-veiled warning that we needed to show something for our efforts.

With the first mate's threat hanging over my head, I called an early end to our break. We boarded the skiffs, grateful to be away from the Spanish. If we weren't able to get to the hold by the end of the day a decision would have to be made. The proper way to salvage her would be to start taking it apart. It was not the best or easiest way to reach the treasure, but the activity would keep them happy—and that was the first step to our freedom.

That evening, after a nonproductive afternoon, I was called to the captain's cabin. The invitation came as a surprise; I knew exactly how small my old cabin was. The reason for the visit became evident when I saw his swollen foot set on a pillow.

"The gout," he said, between sips from a large mug.

"Sorry about that." I had no reason for a conflict and after my own recent injuries, I empathized with the man. "One of my men has a tree bark that helps with the pain."

"I'd be grateful," he said, draining his mug. He banged on the bulkhead and a minute later a man knocked, then entered to refill the mug from a pitcher on the table. The captain looked my way and I nodded, more for wanting to know what he was drinking than actually to drink it. If the captain was incapacitated it might change things topside as we plotted our escape. Excepting his condition, I doubted the captain was a dimwit or inferior officer, but the mate was both eager and overdue. The first mate was on the rise, and in a weakening navy, this could be his chance for promotion.

"Heard you found her." He toasted me with his mug.

"We did, though we're having some trouble getting inside." I saw the questioning look on his face and continued. "She split amidships, causing the decks to cave in on themselves. There's barely room for a man to get inside, let alone light enough to see."

"What are our options?" he sighed, and drank again.

He appeared to be a pragmatic man and was expecting the worst. "There's a boom with a block and tackle rigged to it stored below. If we anchor directly over the wreck, we can use it as a crane of sorts and start taking the ship apart."

"Piece by piece?"

"Right, then. There's no other way." I watched him, knowing he was calculating time and provisions. Returning to Havana empty-handed was not an option. He raised his brow, and I had an answer ready.

"Shouldn't be more than a week, maybe two on the outside." I didn't want to scare him, but he needed to know the truth or it would come back and haunt me later.

"I noticed that contraption you made. Does it work?"

"Actually, quite well."

"The carpenter is handy. I can have him make another if you think it'd speed up the work."

If the carpenter was the same man as the doctor, I hoped he was better with a hammer and nails than with a bone saw. I explained to the captain how the women had made the hoses from sailcloth and we had fashioned the headgear from a bucket and a porthole. "We'll be needing lard and pitch to seal it all."

"There's an island not far off that is covered with pines. We can get you sap for your pitch there. As for the lard, our stores should be enough," he said.

I thanked him, wishing him luck with the gout. On my way

out the door he asked if I could send my African in with some of his bark. I confirmed I would, and leaving the cabin I had a smile on my face, thinking that at least until he needed to be my enemy that I had an ally. That would be important—especially after I stepped up on the companionway stairs and ran straight into the first mate.

Chapter 24

"You and the captain have a nice chat?" he asked, pushing a finger into my chest.

Instead of reacting, which would have given him cause to strike me, I turned sideways to slide by him. Two steps up the ladder I felt a hand grip my shoulder.

"I'd like a word."

"Right, then." I turned back to him.

"Captain's gout has him taking to the drink. I'm not sayin' he's not fit for command, but I'll be watching you carefully."

I nodded, understanding both the threat and the hint of mutiny. He released me, and as I walked back to the hold, I thought about this information. A mutiny aboard would be the worst possible outcome. One that would keep me well away from Havana and Shayla. Whatever I could do to help the captain until we were back in port, I would.

My request to allow the crew to spend the night unfettered had fallen on deaf ears. If the captain wasn't going to help us, there was no point asking the first mate. With the guard following behind me, I climbed down into the hold and allowed him to lock the wrist and ankle irons. I might have gotten mercy for myself, but I'd always thought I should receive no better treatment than my crew. I regretted that decision as the night wore on and I suffered another night with little sleep.

We split our resources in the morning and with Mason in charge of the divers, I set about making another helmet. After our experience making the first one, and with the help of the surprisingly adept carpenter, it went together quickly, but the first mate and crew wouldn't be back until tomorrow with the pine pitch. It had been a small source of amusement to see the mate's unusually foul mood this morning after the captain assigned him the task.

With my work at a standstill and the second skiff and half our men out in search of pine trees to harvest pitch, I called over to the working skiff and asked Mason to pick me up when the divers surfaced. It was crowded without the other skiff for support, but I wanted to be where the action was. Mason was level-headed, and a top-notch navigator, but had little knowledge of dive operations. Rhames was the fighter of the group —not the finder.

"Any luck?" I asked the divers who had just surfaced.

"No, Captain."

They looked defeated. I'd already laid the groundwork with the captain and first mate for what I suspected would be our next step. They had both seemed resigned to having to dismember the wreck. Having lowered their expectations of a quick reward, with the captain in his quarters, and the first mate off finding our pitch, the afternoon might be the perfect time to gather the supplies we needed for our escape.

Thirty minutes later the second diver surfaced, and gave the same report. Gathering the men around, I told them my plan. The looks of frustration turned to determination and I expected by sundown, we would have what we needed.

If this was to be our chance, I decided on making the next dive myself. As well as giving the divers some extra time on the surface, I knew exactly what I wanted to accomplish. With no room aboard the skiff, the diver equipped with the head gear had remained in the water. Sliding in myself, I swam next to him and waited while the men above removed the helmet from the diver's head and placed it on mine. Once it was secured I released my grip on the skiff and dropped to the bottom.

This would be my only dive today, allowing me to take my time. Once on the bottom, I bypassed the stern section the men had been trying to penetrate and went to the forward section. I remembered the feeling on deck when Lafitte's ship had run into the boom. The impact had dragged our ship within feet of capsizing. Now I inspected the damage that had been done to Lafitte's ship firsthand.

I reached the limit of the hoses and had to wait while one of the freedivers relayed my intentions to the skiff. While I waited, I studied the ship as fish swam in and out of the six-foot-wide gash. Even with the planking askew there was still plenty of room to maneuver into the section. I'd stared across the water at the ship for hours when we were in Cozumel, watching and wondering when Lafitte would make his move against us, and recalled it had two skiffs. They had been hung from davits near midships. One was now directly above me and I studied the hull, determining that there had been no damage to it.

I could feel the slack in the line as the skiff moved over my position and when the freediver came down to let me know they were ready to proceed, I pointed up at the small boat. Weighted as I was, there was no way to ascend without help, but unrestrained, the two freedivers had the mobility to reach it. I had outlined my plan on the surface and each knew what to do.

While they went to work on the skiff, I entered the wreck. The layout was familiar and I quickly found the arms locker. Any firearms would be useless after weeks under water. The steel of the cutlasses and daggers might need an edge, but they would be serviceable.

I had expected the padlock on the armory to be intact. Looking around, I found a pulley, which I used to smash against the rusted metal. The shackle broke into several pieces, which dropped to the deck. Pulling the door was the next challenge, as the saltwater'd had its way with the metal hinges. Prying against it, I finally moved it enough to get half my body inside, and using my body for a lever opened the door all the way.

A school of small fish blew past my facemask as I peered inside. The normally organized weapons were scattered on the deck, but within a few minutes I had shuttled enough to the divers waiting at the skiff to arm our men. Laying them in the sand, I looked up and saw the freedivers struggling with the skiff. Thinking the block and tackle used to raise and lower the boats was frozen as well, I searched for an answer, finally deciding that it would require another dive to free it.

With the plan changed, I had one more goal, and reentered the wreck. Even if I could find the carpenter's workshop, it would be a dangerous and difficult task to reach it. Crossing through the galley, I grabbed several knives, and proceeded deeper into the bowels of the ship. With the ship's bow buried in the sand, the open midships allowed light to stream in. Unfortunately, the gash in the hull also allowed sea life to prowl the interior of the wreck.

I had seen this before. From previous dives, I knew that smaller fish loved the protection brought by the tight quarters of the wreck. This was no different. An eel had taken residence already and I could see the antenna of at least a dozen lobsters.

With this much forage available, larger predators lurked in the larger spaces. Passing them by, I found another set of stairs that led into the depths of the ship. The light was fading with every step, making the search more difficult, but I was determined. Before I reached my goal, the growing darkness forced me to abandon the effort. I was discouraged as I retraced my steps, but I still had the knives and hoped one of the smaller ones would help us pick the locks on our chains.

Moving back toward the light, I saw a school of small fish fly toward me. Generally, they would flee after spotting a larger predator, so when the shadow passed in front of the companionway, I froze. My observation was confirmed when I saw the length of the beast as it passed by the opening. Every bit of eight feet, the shark turned and made another pass, as if sensing there were easy pickings close by.

There was nothing to be done except wait it out and hope the shark found an alternative to me for its meal. Creeping toward the opening, I saw no sign of the freedivers. They had stayed outside the wreck, and, unencumbered by gear, had likely bolted for the safety of the surface and the waiting skiff.

The shark made another turn, and I saw one of its cold dark eyes lock onto me. Flicking its tail, the great grey beast closed the gap between us. I backed into the galley, but was quickly jerked forward. Another jerk on the hoses and lines pulled me closer to the exit. I was still inside and protected by the wreck, but detected the cause just as I was slammed against the bulkhead.

The shark, entangled in the hoses and lines, was no longer interested in me. Thrashing its powerful tail, it zigged and zagged in an effort to free itself from its restraints, but with every attempt, it became more tangled. The beast continued to struggle and with every maneuver I was tossed about like a rag doll.

I knew what I had to do and with the blade in my right hand I was about to slash through the lines coming from my helmet when a violent move from the shark slung me against the wreck again, causing me to drop the knife. As I reached for it, I saw movement above, and I looked up in horror as the beams above my head came crashing down on me.

Chapter 25

With its last violent move, the shark had somehow freed itself and disappeared. With my circumstance improved, I checked my body, feeling my extremities. It was all good until I tried to move my legs. Thankfully they were not crushed, but were stuck beneath a large beam. Using what leverage I could, I tried to pull them clear with no luck, and turned my focus on the beam itself. It was a large piece of timber that had spanned the gunwales, giving support for the deck. Fortunately, the beam had caught on something as it fell. Whatever it was had saved my legs. They were pinned down, but not crushed.

The helmet remained intact as well, allowing me to continue breathing as if nothing had happened. I knew there was some relation between deeper water and the diving sickness and I could only hope I was shallow enough that it wouldn't affect me as I waited, knowing sooner or later the divers would be back in the water looking for me.

From my position, I could see the bottom of the skiff and one of the divers as he broke the surface of the water. Still connected to the hoses and lines, I was easy enough to find, but as the man approached the ship creaked loudly and I slashed my hands in front of me warning him to back away. With my heart pounding in my ears, I felt the ship shift behind me, but it stopped and all was quiet again. The diver tentatively approached, and upon reaching me tried to lift the beam. Even with both of us working, our efforts were futile.

Communicating is almost impossible underwater. With the dive bell, we had been able to talk inside the chamber, but with the helmet on, there was no way to tell the diver what needed to be done. From what I could see, the only way out for me was to use the block and tackle aboard the ship to start lifting the debris. Using my hands, I tried to communicate this to the diver. Unsure whether he understood or not, he had exhausted his air supply and headed back to the surface.

The divers changed places, but I waved the replacement off. There was no reason for them to risk their own lives checking on mine. The diver returned to the surface and a few minutes later I saw several men swim off in the direction of the ship. The skiff was my lifeline and needed to remain above me. The wreck continued to shift, making loud noises that reminded me of the sounds my stomach made when it was upset.

Behind me, a large crash brought my attention to the bow, where the deck had caved in on the hold beneath it. A large silt cloud formed as the falling material hit the sand. Looking back, it appeared every cavity that had given the ship its shape was gone. The wreck, which before had risen ten feet from the bottom, now lay more or less flat.

A grating sound broke the surreal quiet. Noises, especially metal against metal, carried a long way underwater, and even though the ship was a hundred yards away I could clearly hear the links of the chain rode clink against each other as the anchor was raised. From the direction of the waves visible on the surface it appeared the wind would carry the ship back to my position, and within a few minutes I saw its large shadow on the surface. The anchor dropped about fifty yards away and the ship settled back just above me.

Except for a small cloud where the anchor had landed, the silt had settled, and with the knowledge that my rescue was in hand I looked around what was left of the forward section of the wreck. The masts and rigging had toppled when the boat originally sunk and were spread out in the sand nearby. The deck had collapsed, leaving several posts and beams all that remained of the forward section. The resident fish, sensing the danger was over, returned, swimming around what looked like a skeleton rising from the ocean floor.

My evaluation was interrupted by a diver in the water. He swam over to check on me, while just past him another man worked the line from the makeshift crane around the topmost piece of wreckage. The diver looped the rope around the highest timber—not the one that lay directly above my legs—a well-thought-out move. Patiently I waited while that beam and the next were raised. As they didn't drop back into the water, I assumed they were hauled aboard the ship. Heavy timber, even seasoned by a month of saltwater, was in heavy demand in an area where the base of the thickest trees was not much wider than my leg.

After lifting everything obstructing it, they finally started on the beam that had trapped me. I soon felt the weight lift and cautiously pulled my legs away. Slowly, I stood and walked several steps. Satisfied I was in good condition, I started toward the now-visible forward hold.

One of the divers swam next to me, probably thinking that I was disoriented, and once he got my attention, pointed up to the ship. I returned his signal, telling him I was alright, and continued forward. Reaching the rubble, I carefully climbed over the deck boards and found myself in the hold. It lay exposed. Lafitte's ship had been assigned as our escort while we recovered the treasure from the *Panther*. As such, they were not provisioned with any trade goods. In fact, the only thing aboard was a third-share of our salvage efforts. Stored in the otherwise-empty hold, the chests were piled near what had been the forward bulkhead.

Separating me from the treasure was a wild array of beams, planks, rigging, and everything else that had been in this section of the ship. What lay in front of me seemed impassable. Even if I could walk through the maze, boards scattered at all angles would surely have snagged the air hose.

The boom we had rigged had taken the ship down, but the coral heads and formations that had further damaged the hull on impact and now projected through the ship's bottom, I wondered if the tactic had even been necessary. Looking around me, I saw several cannon lying nearby. What had once been the gun and main decks of the ship had collapsed. If my plan worked, it might be worth salvaging several, but for now I passed them by. With everything that had happened I needed to get to the surface.

Pulled aboard the skiff, I received a warm reception from the men, but I had too much on my mind to celebrate.

Mason was at the tiller.

"Can you row to the forward section of the wreck?" I asked him.

He gave the order without question and the freedmen at the oars pulled toward the area I pointed to. The sun was dipping into the western horizon, setting some glare on the water, and I would check again from the deck and rigging of the ship when I returned, but for now, I wanted to see what the wreck looked like from the surface. It was flat-calm, the water clear enough that the bottom could easily be seen from the deck of the ship, but it was the level of detail I was interested in. I needed to know if the lookouts aboard the ship could see that the hold now lay open. What I hoped was that the water obscured just enough of the wreck to buy us some time. Now that we knew where the treasure was and how easy it would be to recover it, we could spend a few days biding time and working on my plan to escape.

From the perspective of the skiff it was difficult to see the bottom. I stood, shading my eyes with my hand, and peered into the water. The wreck was visible, but only by its straight lines. Other than the obvious man-made features, there was no telling the condition of the wreck. Once aboard the ship I would evaluate it again.

"I've seen enough. Take us back to the ship, if you please."

Mason gave me one of his looks that made me question if I had lost my mind. His interest in my well-being aside, he would have to wait until later to find out what I had found. For now, I wanted to make a report to the captain before the first mate returned.

Chapter 26

STEVEN BECKER

While I waited for the captain to summon me to his cabin, I saw the second skiff approach the ship. The first mate stood tall in the stern, no doubt giving orders to the men at the oars. Watching him, I couldn't help but think how our leadership styles differed. He got what he wanted from his men through threats, intimidation, and fear; I tried to earn mine. I suspected we would soon get a chance to see whose crew reacted better under duress.

Standing above the hold waiting to see if the captain would call me down before the first mate returned, I winced when I heard the sound of the chains being placed on my men. Vengeance would be ours, but we would have to be patient. We had found the treasure, but our goal was no closer. Tomorrow, while timbers were being brought to the surface, I would make sure we stockpiled the tools and weapons we needed for our escape.

There was still no word from the captain when the first mate climbed over the rail and immediately sought me out. Growing up around pirates, there were few men that intimidated me. The man standing toe-to-toe with me now was one.

It wasn't only his size; there was a look he had about him, a darkness in his eyes, that told me he was no stranger to violence.

"We've done your errand," he said.

I had to bite my tongue for wanting to inform him that any gold retrieved would enrich him more than me. "We'll take it from here. I'll need a few of my men released to do the work."

He nodded to the two men beside him, who climbed down into the hold. A few minutes later, Blue and Mason appeared. We would not only get the hoses prepared, but hopefully, as the guards had become lax, we would have the chance to talk.

"Right, then."

"And what of the diving today?" he asked.

"I was waiting for the captain to summon me. I'll give him a full reporting."

"The captain's indisposed." He cast a mutinous look at the companionway. "You'll give me the damned report."

His tone told me there would be no seeing the captain tonight. "Very well. We had divers below for most of the day. They made little progress, so I went myself this afternoon."

His look eased slightly at my revelation that I had done some of the work. "The stern is totally blocked. The bow less so. We had a problem, though." I told him of my run-in with the shark, and again I could tell his opinion of me rose, if only slightly.

"Wouldn't want to see one of those buggers up close."

"In order to untangle the beams we had the ship brought above the wreck and used the block and tackle. Three or four beams already should be aboard." I was about to say they were worth something in themselves, but he already knew that. The only problem with the lumber was its size. There would be no way to leave them off the manifest, a common ploy for the crew to enrich themselves.

"With two divers, all your men, and mine, we should make short work of it."

I was surprised by his offer to help. The manpower would be welcome, but it would also force our time line. Instead of dragging the salvage operation out for a few days—which would have let us accumulate what we needed for our escape—with both crews working together our preparations would have to be completed tomorrow.

He turned and walked away without another word. While I applied the pitch, finishing the second helmet, Blue and Mason laid out the hoses to start treating them with lard, I thought about the first mate's decision to put his crew to work with us. It would surely be unpopular, leaving me wondering what the reason might be. It had to be time; we had the provisions to stay out for two weeks, which the salvage would have realistically taken—without the shark attack that had inadvertently revealed the treasure. The first mate was no fool. He knew what the bones of a ship looked like, and that if we had brought up four beams in an hour's time, the decks of both halves of the wreck could be cleared tomorrow.

With the helmet finished, we'd been greasing the hoses for an hour in silence. I'd checked every five minutes to see where, and how alert, the guards were. Every time I looked, they were further away. On a ship this size there was only so far one could move and they had reached that limit.

"The deck collapse exposed the forward hold. The chests were sitting there plain as day." Blue's and Mason's faces appeared to be set in stone, knowing better than to expose their true emotions. It would be hard to leave the chests behind, but with the first mate pressing hard, we would have no choice but to execute our plan tomorrow.

"What about weapons?" Rhames asked.

Both men showed more interest in our escape than the gold. Rhames was out for the bloodsport, but I knew Blue would give everything he had to rescue Lucy, as I would for Shayla.

"We've got a pile of cutlasses and daggers in one of the sunken skiffs. We get this second set of gear ready, we can be sending up lumber all day and still strip her of everything that might be valuable."

"Still got the locks on the chains to deal with," Rhames reminded me.

We fell silent for a few minutes while we greased the hoses. I'd never liked that part of the plan. There wasn't a lock-pick amongst us, though Blue had a knack for things like that, but if there was even one lock that we couldn't pick the plan would fail.

"Take the bastards in broad daylight. We's all unlocked then, anyway. If that cock-sure bastard is game to put his crew to work, ain't no of 'em gonna be watchin'."

He was right, but we would surely be noticed salvaging weapons instead of gold. Our plan had called for the bundled weapons to be pulled up to the skiff from the wreck by a line mixed in with the diving equipment. The helmet and hoses were brought aboard every night to be serviced and inspected. The two lines the freedivers used to descend quickly without using their precious air supply were left in place, along with several others used to lower and retrieve tools and treasure. We had taken to leaving those half-dozen lines out. An additional line or two would mean nothing to our captors.

The original plan, as Rhames had pointed out, required the men's locks to be picked—all of them. If we could make the weapons look like they were just another crate of gold, we might be able to smuggle them aboard. Keeping the ship's crew busy salvaging timbers was critical. As I laid out the revised plan, I could only hope that the first mate's unexpected offer of help would benefit us as well.

By the time we were finished talking, the hoses had been

greased twice over. Laying them out to dry, there was nothing to be done except go back to the hold and make the best we could of the rest of the night. What I hoped would be a restful night turned into a soggy mess when the heavens opened at the start of the middle watch, shortly after midnight.

The opened hatch above us allowed the built-up heat of the day to escape and provided us fresh air at night, but no one had anticipated the storm. As typical at these latitudes, it didn't last long, but twenty minutes was plenty of time to thoroughly soak us. What I was worried about—more than the sturdy constitution of the men to endure a little water—was the wind that accompanied the squall and what it might have done to our lines. It was hard to predict what the first mate was going to do under normal circumstances; impossible if something went awry.

Settling back for a cold, wet night, I found that the guards had retreated under shelter, leaving us enough privacy to speak quietly. There was a clear feeling of excitement and fear, as there always is before a battle. I felt it too, but my life held more than just me. There was Shayla, and I had sworn to save her. Part of the pirate image of fearlessness was their day-to-day existence. When you are rich with gold coins in the morning and poor in the afternoon from whoring and gambling, and expect more of the same tomorrow, it's not even worth thinking of the day after, because you might not be alive to witness it. But the men around me, with the exception of Rhames, all had futures that in most cases would include a new family to protect.

Chapter 27

Dawn broke, calm as a sleeping baby. Though as with a child, the weather at this latitude was fickle and could change in an instant, as last night's storm proved. With the squall long gone, it looked like the weather was in our favor—or I hoped so.

"Tomorrow will be a storm."

I turned to Blue, who stood next to me at the rail. He had seen something different in the sunrise and corrected my ignorance.

"Those clouds," he said, pointing to a narrow line of pink clouds high in the sky.

I could see now that they were moving opposite of the larger clouds below. If Blue was right, and he usually was, we would need to accelerate our plan.

With barely a ripple on the water, we loaded into the skiff. The conditions were excellent for supporting the divers and lifting the beams, but without wind to interrupt the surface, it revealed more of the wreck below than I cared to be seen. A lone lookout was perched in the crow's nest above. I feared if he turned and studied the wreck, he would see our ruse, but he

143

was focused on the approaches. If it came, trouble would arrive from that quarter.

After a short meeting with the first mate about the logistics and signals for lifting the beams, the crew and I dropped down to the waiting skiffs. With the ship positioned over the wreck, the skiffs were secured by lines run up to the deck. If all went according to plan they would remain there, serving as platforms to assist the divers.

For our plan to have any chance to succeed it would need the element of surprise. It was alarming to look up to see the first mate staring at us. Proceeding with the recovery effort as if nothing was astir was essential. As badly as I wanted to get in the water, I decided it would be to our benefit if I made only the last dive, ensuring that everything was ready. Bringing the first two divers together, I explained what I wanted them to do.

The first beam broke the surface a half hour later. We had decided on a pace quick enough to keep the crew on the ship occupied and, hopefully, tire them out. Though the diving was often difficult, the heavy lifting would be done on the deck. A steady stream of lumber was hauled up, disguising the activity of the other diver working the wreck. If asked, that could easily be explained as further exploration, but I wasn't inclined to defend my plan.

Toward noon, with the sun directly overhead, I started to worry that with the surface still as a sheet of glass, our covert underwater operations were easily seen. Maybe it was because I knew what the men below were doing that another man could see it for what it was. My impatience finally got the best of me, and I decided to take the next dive rotation.

After sitting in the sweltering sun all morning, the water was cool and refreshing. My fear that our plan would be exposed was quelled when I saw that the morning's work had stirred up the silt, reducing visibility to around twenty feet toward the bow, and even less at the stern, where the beams were being lifted. Not wanting to waste any time, I quickly checked the demolition work, and seeing that there were only a handful of heavy timbers left, I knew we were running out of time.

Moving forward in the wreck, I checked the submerged skiff, which was loaded with weapons. It took thirty minutes to transfer the better ones to the forward hold. Approaching the nearest chest, I met my first obstacle—the padlock. Knowing Lafitte's paranoia, I should have expected this, but the salt-water fortunately had taken its toll, and it fell away when I smashed it to pieces with the hilt of a dagger.

Just to make sure the sun shining from above didn't illuminate any gold, I hovered over the chest as I opened the lid. As I expected, it was full of the gold bars we had twice recovered: first in Haiti, and again from the wreck of the *Panther*. One at a time I removed the bars from the chest, setting them out of sight underneath a coral outcropping that had penetrated the ship. With that phase complete, I loaded the now-empty chest with the weapons. A thought struck me as I started to haul the chest across the deck. Thinking there was nothing like the glitter of gold for a diversion, I stopped and retrieved several bars, which I placed on top of the weapons.

Securing the chest to one of our extra lines, I looked up at the surface. From the sun's angle as its rays penetrated the water, I knew I had overstayed my scheduled time, and made my way underneath the skiff where one of the freedivers relayed to the crew above that I was ready.

I was hauled to the surface where I allowed the men to remove the headgear. After climbing aboard, I told Rhames and Mason that we were ready. Now we just needed an opportunity. We had become quite proficient at raising the beams and I wasn't surprised when a freediver surfaced and told me it was the last one. Checking the sun, I marked that it had been no more than a half hour since I'd surfaced. Experience told me that if I dove again this quickly I would be risking the diving sickness—but I had no choice.

Letting Rhames and Mason know it was time. I asked one of the freedivers to send up the diver working in the stern. He surfaced a few minutes later and I could feel the tension build around me as I readied myself.

"It'll have to be fast. Bring the chest as close to the ship as you can, and as soon as I surface and show them the gold bar, we take it." Even without firepower we had a distinct advantage. The skiffs were secured adjacent to the ship under the flare of the hull. Unless someone leaned over the rail from above with the intent to see what we were doing, we were concealed. I hoped to have all eyes on the gold bar, allowing the men in the skiffs below to arm themselves, climb the ladder, and take the ship. I regretted not being in the vanguard, but to hold the attention of the men above, the reveal of the gold had to be done by me.

Mason, Rhames, and Blue signaled that they were ready, and I slipped over the side. Moving quickly, I reached the stack of gold bars beneath the coral outcropping and took one. Returning to the chest holding our cache of weapons, I gave the signal that I was ready. As I waited to be hauled to the surface, I could see the bottom of the skiffs. One was moved to about fifty feet from the ship. It wasn't much, but if all eyes above were focused on me and the gold bar I carried, they wouldn't strain themselves to see what was happening aboard the other skiff, where the men would be waiting to assault the ship.

I felt a tug on the line, which I returned and felt myself being pulled to the surface. This was the signal for Rhames to haul the chest aboard, arm the men, and start climbing the rope ladder. When I had the Spanish crew's attention, my men would jump the rail and take the ship from the gold-struck crew.

Handing the bar to the freediver to keep it concealed until I was ready, I tried to remain calm while the men in the skiff removed my gear. I climbed aboard and glanced once more at the men climbing the ladder. Rhames was holding the top rung with one hand. With his dagger between his teeth and the cutlass in his free hand, he smiled as our eyes met. I nodded and climbed aboard the skiff.

Leaning over the side, I took the bar from the freediver and called up to the men watching from above. I needn't have spoken, as the gold did the work for me. Seconds later a cheer went up and all hands were leaning over the rail looking at me.

We had positioned the skiff forward of the rope ladder, and with every man aboard, including the first mate, staring at the gold bar, Rhames and the men were invisible as they silently climbed onto the deck.

Chapter 28

Minutes later, when one of the men signaled from above that it was clear, and with the line still securing us to the ship, we pulled ourselves to the ladder. I reached for the rung just above me and quickly climbed to once again set foot on deck as the captain.

So complete was their surprise that most surrendered without a fight. The exception was the still defiant first mate. He had the most to lose by the insurrection and fought back. As I climbed over the rail, I saw the mate on his knees. Rhames was toying with him and finally, on seeing me, took one swat to the man's head with the blunt edge of the cutlass. The blow knocked the first mate to the deck and a small pool of blood formed by him, the only bloodshed.

It was a simple matter for Mason and the crew to place the prisoners in the same chains that only this morning had restrained us. The first mate was last to be unceremoniously tossed down and secured. That left only the captain.

Our insurrection had been a quiet affair, and not surprisingly the captain was nowhere to be seen. As I headed to the companionway, Rhames started to follow, but I turned him back. I knew it would take the old pirate a good night of drinking before the bloodlust faded.

"Let me handle this captain-to-captain. I have a suspicion that the first mate was planning a mutiny, and I think I can convince the captain of it. That'll give us the cover we need to sail into Havana."

He let me go, and as I descended the stairs to the lower deck I heard him berating the first mate. My strategy continued to evolve with every step I took, and I had to admit it wasn't fully formed when I knocked on the door.

"Enter," the captain called out.

I opened the door to see him in the same position as the previous visit. A quick look confirmed his continued bad health. Though Blue's bark medicine had relieved some of the pain, he had refused further treatment. Now that I had control of the ship, I would insist on it. One of the freedmen lurked in the shadows of the passageway in case I needed anything. I called back to him to bring Blue.

"It appears there was an attempted mutiny on deck. My men quelled it and we have your first mate and crew in chains."

Before the captain could answer, Blue appeared in the doorway.

"I'll not take that witch doctor's potions."

I looked at the man, trying to establish how sick he really was. Keeping him alive was of paramount importance. Without the captain to confirm the mutiny, our plan would be ruined and instead of heroes we would be the mutineers. Studying the man, I couldn't help but notice his inflamed foot. I nodded at Blue, who approached the captain. Handing him a piece of the bark, which the captain accepted, he placed a poultice of the fish weed on his swollen foot. Now that the captain had accepted Blue's medicine, I hoped to iron out the details of our story.

"Before you decide what to do, I need to tell you that the mutiny was real. The first mate implied several times that you were too infirm to act in your assigned capacity."

"He was always the officer you had to hold down."

It appeared that he was feeling some relief from his pain as his mouth worked the bark between words.

"We found the gold as well. You'll be returning a hero."

"Nothing like turning over a pile of gold to the governor." He looked down at his foot. "Your witch doctor have any more of that magic?" he asked with a smile.

I expected we had an agreement, and left him in Blue's care, agreeing to return with news of the treasure. As I left I had a few words with the freedman outside the door. Even with the captain's infirm condition, I made sure to give orders to the man now standing guard. The door was to remain open and he was to remain vigilant. There were likely weapons in the cabin, but between my desire for the captain to save face and his lack of mobility, I had decided not to perform a search. My explanation to the captain was that the man was there if he needed anything, but the guard was armed and the story was just a shallow pretense for his presence.

Climbing back to the deck, I glanced at the position of the sun and, seeing it was a hair over four fingers above the horizon, decided with an hour before dark to dive again. The chance of another ship stumbling upon us was remote but, if one did, we stood to lose everything we had gained. To be safe I posted a lookout then gave Mason command of the ship.

Pulling Rhames aside, I put him in charge of the prisoners with express orders that they were not to be harmed. He cast a look at the first mate and I confirmed my order included him.

Gingerly, I dropped down the ladder to the skiff, the sun was another finger closer to the horizon, meaning we had fifteen minutes less daylight to work with. I called up to the men manning the block and tackle to see if they were ready, and when they confirmed, the divers dropped into the water. The crates containing the treasure had fittings bolted to them, making it easy work to hook them up, and I expected with two divers and we could complete the task by sunset.

"Sail!"

The lookout's call changed everything. Ceasing diving operations, I had the men wait while I scurried up the ladder to the deck. I didn't stop until I stood on the top spar next to the lookout. Without a word, pointing toward a spot on the horizon, the lookout handed me the glass. I could see only a spec without it and vowed to remember to praise the man later for his vigilance. With the glass to my eye I could clearly see the ship. From the direction of its wake, I could tell it was coming towards us.

Darkness would have saved us, except for the black sails the ship flew—a sure sign it was pirates, and they wouldn't stop for the night. Evaluating our situation, I called down for the divers and skiffs to be brought aboard. Retrieving the skiffs would cause us time and work to reposition them, but there was little choice.

"Recover the gear and toss the lines." I was not going to lose the gear or give another ship the location of the wreck by leaving buoys on the surface.

The question was how experienced the pirate captain was with these waters. If he was to sail straight toward us there would be no reason to move, as they would founder on the reef. As appealing as that option was, any captain or navigator sailing here knew the danger. What we needed was to reach open water, and fast.

"Haul the anchor as soon as the skiffs are secure," I called down to the deck.

Mason looked up and I pointed toward the bow, in the direction of the narrow cut. We had navigated through it once before, and I was sure we could do it again. Faced with a choice of having to navigate the shoals back toward Garden Key, I chose open water. My plan was to wait until the pirate ship committed to her course, then make a run for it.

I climbed back up and exchanged the glass back and forth with the lookout while the ship was readied beneath me. The first skiff had been secured and the block and tackle were being lowered for the second. The pirates maintained course, a move I didn't understand. Leaving the glass with the lookout, I climbed down to the deck.

I found Mason as confused as I, bent over the chart table studying the other ship's approach. "Can't make sense out of their course."

Looking up, I could see the ship clearly now. Something about it seemed familiar. It took me a second, and then it came to me. It was one of Lafitte's fleet. There had been survivors from the wrecks. At least someone aboard the approaching ship knew these waters.

"Lafitte's men," I said, and saw the recognition in Mason's face. At the mention of the pirate's name, Rhames was by our side. "She holds her course, she'll be on us."

"Keep the activity to a minimum, but prepare for battle and fly all sail."

Lafitte's ship was coming up the wide anchorage that funneled past *The Tongue* and into the narrow channel. Already anchored In the confines of the pass, we were in no position to turn and face them. We would have to run, and if that were the case, we had to go now.

"Hoist the anchor. All sail." The ship became a flurry of activity. Rhames was with the men at the capstan, driving them hard around the winch that slowly pulled the chain aboard. Straining against the rode, the ship with all sails flying was chomping at the bit. When they finally freed the anchor, she took off.

The ship healed hard to port as the sails filled, catching

Mason off-guard. He called out several course corrections, which were cleanly and quickly executed. Everyone aboard knew the danger we were in. Finally, the ship straightened and, though it was too dark to see them, I could feel the coral heads below us a they came within inches of our hull. There wasn't a breath taken until we cleared the channel and then only a small one as we all looked back and saw the black sails beating down on us.

Chapter 29

There was a reason pirates used black sails, and as the sun dropped below the horizon it was evident. As the slow burn of twilight settled around us, the ship was invisible from the deck. Calling up to the lookout, I got the same response. As I looked back, I saw nothing but water—except the Spanish flag flying from our stern gave me an idea. The quicker we approached Spanish waters, the likelihood of Lafitte's ship following was reduced with every mile.

Making my way to the binnacle, I approached Mason. "We need to reach Spanish waters." Due to the shoals surrounding us and then the current in the Straits, I knew the straightest line was not always the most expedient route.

"Aye, for once we've got a country looking after us."

We did, as long as the captain would go along. "I need to check on the captain. You've got command," I said to Mason. Rhames had a knack for appearing whenever certain words were used: gambling, weapons, and anything to do with command. He appeared now at my side.

"I'll see to the weapons. Damned Spanish probably have the guns all buggered up."

With Mason and Rhames occupied, I made my way to the captain's cabin. The door was open as I had requested and the guard nodded to me as I entered. The change was evident the minute I set foot in the cabin. The captain sat up. There was a bottle in front of him, but it looked untouched.

"You're looking better."

"Much, thanks to Blue here. I was just about to go on deck and see what I can get out of that first mate of mine."

I told him about the ship in pursuit. His demeanor changed and he rose, only to fall back into the chair. "You wouldn't think a damned toe would give you this much trouble."

"There's nothing to be done for now." I promised to keep him informed. I would at some point have to tell him he was no longer in command. I'd hoped that conversation would wait until we passed the fortresses guarding the entrance to the harbor. Taking my leave, I asked Blue to conjure up something to make the captain sleep.

The guard stepped aside as I passed. I asked him to notify me immediately if the captain tried to leave the cabin. "Just don't treat him like a prisoner," I said as my parting words.

"But he is then, isn't he?" the guard asked, confused.

Pulling him into the passageway, I explained our predicament and he nodded his head in understanding. He returned to his post at the doorway. On my way to the deck, I stopped to check the armaments. I stood to the side and watched Rhames working with the two Scotsmen. They wouldn't replace Red and Swift, whose chances of surviving the cooking pot on Harp's deck decreased with every day. The thought only furthered my sense of urgency.

"Squared away then," Rhames said proudly. "Let the bastards sidle up to us and we'll show them what."

Here was an idea that hadn't occurred to me. As the pirates had with their black sails, we, too, could use the night to our favor. "Black out the ship. We go dark."

"Aye, the bastards'll never know what hit'm."

That would wait to be seen, but he would be ready if need be. Rhames left to give the orders and in short order, I could barely see my hand in front of my face. With a new moon and enough cloud cover to hide the stars, it was a dark night, perfect for our ploy. The only problem was the potential for a collision. With the gold aboard, sinking in the deep water of the Straits would leave it well beyond our reach.

Rhames had warned the men to hold the noise down and when he returned, I was taken by surprise at his stealth. "Been taking lessons from Blue?"

"Little bugger's crafty, ain't he? Ship's dark and quiet. We have any idea where the pirates are?"

"I'll go have a look." Sound carried a long way over the open water and seemed to even more so at night. Leaving Rhames and the Scotsmen to their preparations, I climbed the mast and stood next to the lookout. "Any sign of them?"

"Over there." He pointed to a dark spot on the water.

Focusing on the spot, I saw the bioluminescence of their ship's wake as it closed on our position. I knew firsthand after our visit to his enclave that Lafitte had several fast ships. The vessel itself was invisible, but the disturbed seas behind it were plainly seen. Looking at our stern I could see the same phenomena. "Keep a sharp eye," I told the lookout and climbed back to the deck. Rhames saw me descend and followed me to the binnacle.

"They're back there. Look closely and you can see their wake."

Mason immediately grasped the situation and ordered the crew to drop all but the foresails. The triangular sails would give us enough headway to steer and were capable of sailing at all aspects except directly into the wind. "They're likely to be on us within the hour. We should come about before they can see us."

"Aye," Mason said, and called out the orders.

With most of our canvas lashed to the spars it was a slow maneuver but, for our plan, I preferred stealth to speed. Finally, the ships were bow to bow. There was no indication that we had been seen and I could feel the tension build as the gap between us closed. Rhames went from man to man explaining the signals he would use. Hand gestures would be of no use on the dark deck and even more invisible below. Instead, he used a clicking sound he made with his tongue. The idea was for each man to repeat it to the next.

"The men and guns are ready," Rhames whispered, "If the damned Scotts don't bugger up the signal."

"Small arms?"

Even in the darkness I could see his smile.

"Bet that bastard first mate has the key." He left to retrieve it.

I only hoped he would do so quietly. Mason and I stood by the helm, watching as the wake of the ship behind us signaled her approach. There was still no sign we had been spotted when I asked Mason to drop whatever sail was left. Confident we were on a collision course, the sails, though small, could still reflect light.

We were adrift and at the mercy of the seas, but there was no other course. Mason had calculated the current and assured me that we would crab to the side as the ship approached. As it was, our bow pulpits would meet. Bracing myself for the coming carnage, I found Rhames and told him to prepare.

He had two pistols and fresh, clean steel in his belt, clearly ready for action. "Sink'em, take their masts down. Whatever you have to do. Use the small arms across the rails, but we can't afford to be boarded," I told him. I had no idea what numbers we faced and a fight on our deck in the dark of night could go either way.

Looking around, I realized Blue was still below with the

captain. "I'm going after Blue."

"Bugger's good help in a fight," Rhames said.

The ship was so quiet I could hear my footfalls as I climbed down the stairs and made my way to the captain's cabin. Dismissing the man at the door with directions to find Rhames, I entered the cabin.

"This character of yours is quite interesting."

Blue sat in a chair across the table, smiling. "We're coming up on the pirate ship, or she's actually coming up on us," I explained our tactic to the captain.

"Makes sense. We've not got the fastest ship in the fleet."

She was considerably slower before we careened her, but she was still an old, heavy ship. Another captain on another ship might discard ballast to lighten her in an attempt to pick up a few knots, but our cargo was a bit more valuable than stone.

"I'll be needing Blue. You're welcome to come on deck or ride it out here. Either way, we'll know soon enough."

The captain got up and tested his foot. I could see the pain in his face as he took his first step, but he seemed to be able to walk and followed me up to the deck. As soon as we felt the fresh air on our faces, we could hear the other ship moving through the water. Hurrying to the binnacle, I left the captain to make his own way, then thought better of it and sent a man back to help him. If we escaped the pirates we still needed him to gain access to the harbor in Havana.

Just as I reached the binnacle, I heard the first click. The deck was soon awash in the sound, and a second later, the cannon on our port side fired. The brief flash of light from the powder gave me a few seconds to watch as the unsuspecting ship was broadsided. Before I could evaluate the cannonball's effectiveness, thick smoke overwhelmed us, but it didn't obscure the screams of injured men and the crash as the other ship's mast fell.

Chapter 30

I'd been in enough battles to know anything can happen and the outcome is seldom what you'd planned. In this case, I couldn't have been happier. With one broadside the battle seemed to be over. Their mast had come down, of that I was sure. Whether the ship had sunk or not, I didn't know or care. She was in no condition to follow us, and after likely being swept north and east, would be a victim of the Gulf Stream's quick current.

Worried about retaliation, Mason had laid on all sail as soon as the shots had been fired and we were moving quickly toward safety. The mood about the ship was good, including the captain, who brought a private bottle from his cabin that he passed around between Rhames, Mason, and I. Before Rhames could get his fill, and under the disapproving eye of the captain, I walked amongst the crew sharing the brandy with them.

"That's an expensive bottle to be passing around," the captain said, when I returned.

"If not for the men, we wouldn't be drinking it," I said, handing the remnants to Rhames, who downed it in one gulp.

STEVEN BECKER

The subject wasn't worthy of an argument that would sour the mood, and I walked away, ending any discussion of the matter.

Time has a way of standing still during conflict and when I saw sky turn dark purple, and then the thin line of dawn on the horizon, I was surprised. After relieving the lookout, thanking him again for his focus, I stayed aloft. For all their bravado, pirates could be a fearful lot and many were scared of the waters we sailed on, as well as the height of the masthead. My size and agility had me climbing the rigging at a young age. Even as captain, with my own cabin, I felt more at peace up there. The wind brushing against my skin rarely failed to put a smile on my face.

In the growing light, I studied the water behind us, confirming with the aid of the glass what my naked eye saw—nothing. As I put the glass down, the bell rang signaling the morning watch and I was soon relieved. Climbing down, I went to the binnacle to check on our progress and reported seeing no sign of the enemy ship.

"Reckon we'll be in sight of land around noon. Enter the harbor on the evening tide," a bleary-eyed Mason said.

I could see he had been up all night, as had I, and needing him alert to negotiate the entrance to the harbor, relieved him for a few hours rest. After a thorough briefing of our heading and course, as well as the conditions and weather—most of which I knew—he reluctantly headed below. The deck was quiet, with only the men on watch present. Wanting to have a fresh and alert crew when we entered Havana, I ordered the morning to be split into two dog-watches. The two-hour shift would allow all the men at least some rest.

The morning passed without incident or sign of the captain. As Mason had predicted, the peaks of the inland mountains appeared as the second watch ended. Mason took back command of the ship and I headed below to visit the captain. It was past time he committed to our plan.

160

Pounding on the door, I realized my mistake when there was no answer. The lever on the handle turned, but the door refused me. He had thrown the bolt. I had an inclination what he was about, but there was also the chance his sickness had gotten the better of him. After knocking for another minute, I stepped back and with my good leg kicked high on the door. The bolt snapped, allowing me entry.

The first thing I saw was the empty bottles scattered on the floor. The table was a mess of spilled wine, and laying half on the bed and half on the floor was the captain. It took a forceful shove to elicit any response from him, and that was only a twisted scowl and some words muttered in Spanish. Disgust overwhelmed me, as did the stink of him, and I stepped out of the room, glad for the cleaner air of the passageway.

Approaching the harbor under Spanish colors would allow us entry, but with the original crew chained in the hold and no sign of the captain, if we were boarded there was bound to be trouble. I needed him awake and presentable. Leaving the door ajar to air the stench from the cabin, I went back on deck and found Blue.

"The captain's in his cups."

He giggled, not understanding the gravity of the situation. Not a drinker, he enjoyed an occasional pipe of tobacco or the weed they grew in Jamaica. The escapades of the crew when drink was abundant, especially Rhames and the other pirates, was a source of amusement to him. Reminding him that Lucy's life depended on the captain's behavior over the next few hours sobered him.

"Leave him to me," Blue said.

I ordered one of the freedmen to go with him, with directions to bathe and dress the captain.

"What time do you think we'll make port?" I asked Mason.

"Sometime around sunset. The rate we're going, we'll have to wait outside the harbor for the flood tide."

"Let's ease off a bit." I explained about the captain's condition. "If we can reach an anchorage as it's getting dark, we can likely avoid a visit until morning." I knew the warden would get word of our arrival from the lookouts at the fort. A fast horse would alert him before we reached the inner harbor. Again, darkness would be our friend.

"How do you intend to get the women back?" he asked.

With everything that'd happened over the last few days, I hadn't given it much thought. My original plan was to pull into port with a load of treasure; now we had the single gold bar I had brought to the surface and what lay buried in the bilge. We were on a personal errand for Blue and I. I'd need the blessing of the crew to dip into our reserves.

Leaving the helm, I went in search of Rhames to ask his opinion. Having him on my side usually was a sure sign that the crew would follow.

Chapter 31

STEVEN BECKER

We slipped through the pass shortly after sunset and found an anchorage just outside of the inner harbor. Mason called out for the rode to be secured after allowing for only short scope—in case we needed a quick exit. Fortunately, it was a pleasant night and in twenty feet of water, the normal eighty feet of rode would have been safe, but with the watch already doubled in case we had any unwanted visitors, we settled on half that. The short length of chain and south wind would give us an easy exit in the event of trouble.

Just as the ship settled back, I saw the captain emerge from the companionway.

"Fine evening," he said, as he approached. "Thought I saw the forts as we entered."

"Right, then. Your health looks to have improved." I doubted he could have walked on his own earlier.

"Your man is a miracle worker." He took a piece of the bark Blue used for pain from his mouth.

"Glad it worked out for you." With his present mood, I thought it was the best time to press for his cooperation. "What do you plan to do with the mutineers?"

He gave me a queer look, and I thought for a second I had overplayed my hand. Rhames, who had been lurking in the background, came up behind me. Hoping the captain didn't see me do it, I gave him a low hand-signal that everything was alright. He saw it and backed off just a bit, but stayed within earshot.

"Hang," he said, cavalierly.

I still wasn't sure if he was talking about us or his crew. "There's the matter of our women."

"I expected that was your aim, bringing the ship back here. Gutsy move, that."

I relaxed slightly, thinking he had been toying with me.

"There is the matter of the treasure."

Recovering it had been our original deal, which we had essentially failed, but we still had Shayla, plus my share of what lay in the keel, which was near half. Add Lucy and Blue's share, and it was close to seventy percent. I would gladly give all mine, and I guessed Blue would agree. "We did recover some," I lied.

He removed the bark from his mouth, spit out a chunk, and replaced it. "That makes things a bit more interesting."

"Let me get the ship settled and I'll have it brought up." The glitter of gold always helped.

From his expression as he surveyed the harbor I had the feeling he was glad to be home, and alive. It might not take as much gold as I first expected.

"I'll be in my cabin—unless there's too much to fit."

His voice was laced with hopeful sarcasm, "A sample and accounting, then," I teased, as he walked away.

Once he was clear of the companionway I called Blue over. Our discussion was short, but I needed to confirm I could offer his and Lucy's stake. Gathered around the binnacle, I quietly told Rhames and Mason, as the old crew was within earshot, of my willingness to part with our treasure. It was really a matter of courtesy, as each man knew they could have their share had they requested it. It was the next part that worried me.

"If it's not enough, I'd like your permission to use whatever we have. I'll of course guarantee it and pay some interest."

"Your word is all I need. That and enough for a bit of a party next time we find a port that'll take us," Rhames said.

"Mason?"

"Whatever you need."

I could tell he offered it reluctantly, but I wouldn't press him in front of the crew. "Right, then." I gave orders to have a third brought up in two chests.

Extracting hundreds of pounds of gold from deep in the bowels of the ship took some time, and it was close to an hour later when I stood in front of the captain's door with half a dozen men and three chests. Nodding to the freedman again who was charged with the captain's wellbeing, he knocked on the door and I entered. The men followed behind, setting the chests on the floor.

Though he had appeared sober on deck, the captain was again in his cups. Bringing the bottle to his lips, he drank deeply before setting it down. Ribbons of liquid ran down from his mouth to his neck, landing on his already saturated blouse.

"That's what you've got, then?" he slurred.

His condition reminded me that he was not a man to be trusted, which would make negotiation more difficult. I thought about leaving it until the morning, but it might be noon before he rose on his own. We were in plain sight of the forts and I fully expected a customs boat just after first light. This had to be decided now.

I had a feeling where he was headed. "And another like it for yourself."

"We didn't find it, did we?"

I waited to see how he played his hand, wondering if my

ruse had failed. But would it matter? I gave him a look that could go either way.

"Gold is gold. I suppose I shouldn't be too particular as to its origin?"

"We get our women and the ship," I confirmed the terms of the deal.

He picked up the bottle and drank with the same messy result, then handed it to me. I knew it would be a mistake to rebuff him. Taking the bottle I took a swig, spitting as much back as I could before returning it to him. We said goodnight, and I headed back to deck.

With Shayla so close, I doubted I could sleep and sent one of the watches to bed. Climbing to my spot on the top spar, I stared out at Havana. Looking back over our stern at the city, my senses were inflamed with the lights, smells, and sounds. After spending most of the last dozen years at sea or on Gasparilla Island, city life was unfamiliar to me, but enticing. I could almost understand why Rhames and his men were always anxious to reach a friendly port.

The city was alive, but the harbor was generally quiet, with only a few skiffs running back and forth to the boats at anchor. We were close to getting Shayla and Lucy back, and I realized I had no further plan than to escape the Caribbean—the island-speckled sea that held us prisoner to our pasts. Shayla and I had agreed the only way to a legitimate life was to exit its waters. The plan was not without obstacles, though.

Our vessel, though old and slow, was generally seaworthy once her pumps, which we had cannibalized for the dive operations, were restored. Men had sailed worse vessels. Funds were low, but when we made it across to the isthmus, there were hundreds of miles of deserted coastline where we could hunt or fish, though these were uncharted waters. One last bit of business might solve both of those problems: Harp.

While I stood watch, I pondered the question of whether it

was piracy to pirate a pirate, for that is what I intended to do, if we could find him. Slowly, my mind started to drift and I jerked myself awake before I fell asleep. Climbing down to the deck I sought out Mason, both to see what his reluctance had been earlier, and his opinion on Harp's whereabouts. I expected him to be in his bunk or amongst the men scattered on the deck enjoying the fresh air, but I found him at the place where I should have started my search.

Studying the chart spread out on the binnacle, he pulled in a long toke on his pipe, held the tobacco for a second, and released it into the humid night air.

"You never smoke when we are underway, do you?" I asked him.

"Nothing'll do a ship in faster than a fire." He looked up at me. "I'm expecting we'll need to be making a quick exit."

It was a statement, one that bothered me, for it always seemed that we were on the run from one thing or another. "I expect."

"In any event," he drew in again and, touching the map, moved his finger around the eastern tip of the island. Blowing the smoke out, he paused. "It'll be more miles, but for most of the way we'll have the current. Might have to beat into the trades if they hold till we get around the point, but it'll be smooth sailing from there."

He'd said it with conviction, as if he had studied every option, which he had.

"Right, then."

"And, if you want that Englishman and his ship, they'll be here." His finger landed on the two smaller Cayman Islands.

Chapter 32

Of my crew, there were two men and two women who I never questioned, and Mason was one of them. The others were Blue, Lucy, and Shayla. Rhames and his lot would, as pirates do, make decisions on a whim. I was coming to know and like the freedmen, but trust took time and temper; more of both than our short time together allowed. The Scots appeared to have blended in, but I was far from trusting them.

The captain had proven to be about as reliable as one of Rhame's throws of the dice that often got the pirate in trouble, but the man was our best play. Taking Shayla and Lucy back by force was beyond our reach in a city that none of us knew well. With those thoughts rolling around in my head, I suffered a sleepless night, spending my time between the helm and top spar.

The harbor was already busy when the first rays of sunlight hit the water. At least as far as the weather gods were concerned it would be a good day. Unfortunately, their rule ended for the most part where water met land. Despite the previous night's libations, the captain appeared early, dressed for shore carrying all the pomp you would expect from a Spanish officer. There was no point in waiting, and we briefly paused by the rail to confirm and work out the logistics of the trade. He wanted to go ashore alone in the skiff, obtain Shayla and Lucy, and bring them back in return for the treasure.

Things were never so simple. First was the matter of needing our crewmen to row the skiff. That was overcome by swapping uniforms with several of the Spaniards in the hold. Second was what to do with the mutineers, especially the first mate. The lot of them needed to be put off, but I did not want to have them shuttled by the Spanish forces, or to dock and offload them. Tied to the wharf, surrounded by our enemies, we could easily be taken.

There was one constant in the equation: the captain's greed. He wouldn't do anything to jeopardize his new-found riches. Finally, we agreed that the Scots would accompany him to shore. I carefully instructed them in the expected behavior of the Spanish sailors that they were supposed to be representing, and was surprised they almost looked the part—as long as they didn't speak, they'd be fine. Their orders were to make sure the captain spoke to no one other than the warden. They might catch no more than a few words of what was being said, but these two seemed to have an extra awareness when it came to self-preservation.

Staring at the city, a feeling of helplessness came over me as I watched the two freedmen row the group toward the pier. I thought I should have gone myself, but it was too much of a risk. All I could do was wait, and after setting watches on all quarters, I went below to secure what would be left of our treasure if everything went smoothly. I was glad I checked, as I found the remaining gold ballast exposed, with the stones we had used to conceal it arranged in dangerous, unbalanced piles port and starboard. One wave, taken badly, would have toppled them, causing massive and possibly devastating damage to the ship.

Back on deck, I called for Rhames and asked him to oversee a crew to re-stack the ballast, then climbed into the rigging. It was either climb or pace the decks, and that tended to make the crew more nervous than they already were. From my position high above the water, I waited for what felt like an eternity until finally I was saw Shayla's blaze of auburn hair in a skiff being rowed through the harbor. It crossed behind an anchored ship before I could count heads, but my heart jumped just knowing she was alive.

The captain had kept his word, and after waiting as they were rowed across the harbor, Shayla and I had a passionate but brief reunion, then we loaded the promised gold.

"What of your crew?" I asked him.

"Feed the bastards to the sharks for all I care. I'm retired now." He patted one of the chests sitting beside him in the low-riding skiff.

Expecting this, over the last few hours I had come up with a solution. The beach where we had careened the ship several long weeks ago was easily accessible at high tide, and unguarded. It was in the wrong direction, but we could put them ashore there. Mason came beside me, reading my mind as the captain was rowed to a waiting carriage by the docks.

"Change of plans, then?"

"Just a bit. We'll put them ashore where we careened her."

"For the best. Far enough from town, we'll be long gone before they can set an alarm."

"If anyone believes them." I knew this wasn't true. The captain planned to disappear with the gold, making our only friendly witness unavailable. When the word of a Spanish crew was measured against that of a mixed rabble of pirates, we would be hanged if caught.

Just as I thought it, Mason called for sails and a minute

later, the ship tugged against the anchor rode. The crowded harbor had little room to maneuver, and as soon as the men at the capstan freed the anchor, we quickly moved toward the two forts guarding the entrance of the harbor. A bit of luck brought us between them just as the sun set, making visibility difficult, allowing us to sail straight through without incident.

Turning west, we found deep water and changed course to run parallel to the coast. As the forts faded from view, I felt some of the tension leave my body; the rest would remain until we offloaded our prisoners. A movement on the spar distracted me as Shayla joined me.

"You've got a story to tell?" she asked, reaching out to caress my face.

"I do, but I'd like to get up the coast a bit and lose our hostages."

"Can't say I blame you for that. Just want to say thank you."

Though separated by several feet lest we unbalance the spar, I felt as close as I ever had to her. "I'd give anything for you."

"I love you, Nick Van Doren, and I've got a bit of a surprise."

We locked eyes.

"I'm pregnant."

It was the last thing I expected, but as soon as the words were out of her mouth, I knew it was the thing I wanted most. I couldn't speak; instead, I leaned in and kissed her deeply, nearly upsetting our balance. It was a long kiss, a happy kiss, but when we finally separated all I could think of was what lay ahead before we could truly be a family.

"Lucy knows. Of course she sniffed it out. So, if Blue knows, the rest of the crew does as well."

Blue was a master of many things, but keeping a secret was not one of them. I always knew when he had something to tell, as his cheeks puffed out as if he were about to blow a dart.

"We'll get married, then?"

"Right, then, Mr. Van Doren. We will, but first we need to escape these vile waters."

We stayed together both lost in our own thoughts watching the darkened outline of the island as we sailed past. Many islands in the northern Caribbean were flat and bare, but Cuba had a unique coastline outlined by her inland mountains. The moon gave enough illumination to see where we were, and I thought I spied the beach where we had careened the ship.

"There it is, then." I pointed to the spot. Shayla confirmed it, and we both climbed down. It was time to offload our cargo.

I felt ten pounds lighter when my feet hit the deck, and I could see by the looks on the men's faces as they turned toward Shayla and I that they knew—possibly before me.

"Right, then. Rhames!" I called the old pirate over and we discussed the best way to get the men to the beach.

"Be safer during the day," he said.

Rhames liked to see his targets. "Tonight. See that it happens." He turned with a mischievous smile.

"And no blood," I warned him. His plans for revenge against the first mate exposed, his shoulders sagged slightly as he walked off.

I looked at Shayla, about to ask her to climb back into the rigging and keep watch, but suddenly stopped, thinking about my baby in her belly.

"Oh no, you don't," she called me out.

Holding my breath as she climbed, I released it when she was secure in her perch. Having someone aboard with Lucy's skills was a godsend. At the first opportunity, once our cargo was discharged I planned on consulting her. With Shayla safe above, I went to the helm.

"Be good to get rid of them vermin," Mason said, as I approached.

"No problem in the dark?"

He looked around. "Bright as a baby's face." He gave me his crooked smile, telling me he knew as well.

"Right, then. Let's get this bit of business finished."

Just as I said it, I heard a scream from the hold.

Chapter 33

STEVEN BECKER

UNCHARTED
Waters

Rhames had a smug look on his face. "I know what you told me, but the bastard bit me."

A trickle of blood dripping from his mouth, the first mate lay unconscious on the deck.

"Right, then. Get them out of here." Being stacked in the hold for several days had dehumanized them. Instead of dealing with people, I found myself looking at problems, and was beginning to understand the tendency that pirates had for killing their captives.

We were hove-to in fifty feet of water about a quarter mile off the coast. It would have been easier to dispose of the prisoners if we had anchored closer, but we were in enemy waters. If they found us, being pinned against a lee shore would mean certain death. The row through the breakers was longer, but our foremost priority had to be a quick escape if needed. On our starboard side, the open sea beckoned, and I couldn't wait to be free of the island.

The instant the skiff returned from its last trip I could feel the relief spread through myself and the crew. Mason called out an order. The sails snapped, picking up the wind, and we started to move, the ship feeling lighter than the collective weight of the Spaniards we had disembarked.

The current running the opposite direction of our course through the Straits of Florida made it necessary to hug the landmass, which haunted us until noon the next day, when we finally broke free of its grasp. Mason executed a wide turn around the *Banco de San Antonio*, where for the second time in a week we left behind riches under our keel. I knew the cargo of the ship that Harp had sunk lay below us, but the location was too well-traveled to make recovery viable. When the *Isle de los Pinos* finally dropped below the horizon, the burden of the past weeks dropped from my shoulders. There was still the matter of Red and Swift, but there was nothing I could do about it at the moment.

With nothing but open water until we reached the Caymans, and badly needing sleep, I left the ship in Mason's hands. Crossing the threshold of our cabin, hoping for nothing but peace and quiet, I saw the space had been turned into a sewing room, with Shayla and Lucy consumed in the manufacture of baby clothes. Not wanting to disturb them, I went back on deck, found a comfortable place by the bowsprit, and lay down. They say fair winds and following seas are a sailor's dream, and in this case, with the gentle breeze behind us, the ship rolled with the long swell, which soon had me fast asleep.

Several times I awoke, but nothing had changed. Discharging the prisoners and leaving Cuba behind had left the crew feeling the relief and exhaustion that often followed a battle. It takes longer for some than for others, but when the tension leaves your body, there is nothing to do but sleep. Feeling I'd had my share of slumber, I rose, and walked back to the binnacle, stopping at the cask of water for a drink.

"I'd forego the dog watches and give them a bit more rest." The two watches between four in the afternoon and eight in the evening were two hours, rather than four, allowing the crew's schedule to shift every day. Making the afternoon and evening watches six hours each would be welcome.

"Place a keen eye above. Unless we see a sail, I'd cut it in half as well."

I could see the deep lines in Mason's face as he spoke and I expected a mirror would show that I looked the same. "I'll relieve you for the next watch. Get some rest."

Mason nodded and left without a fight. It was unusual for him, but unless something changed, our course would be a dead run southeast for a hundred-twenty miles. If the present conditions held, we would sight the two small islands mid-afternoon tomorrow. Until then, the best thing I could do was to make sure the crew was well-rested. Whether we found Harp or not, the hundreds of miles we planned on traveling past those islands were uncharted waters for all of us.

There was one area of concern. Our exit from Havana had left us no time to provision. Lashing the wheel, I called to one of the freedmen to man the helm while I went below to check out stores. We'd originally been outfitted for a week with essentially a double crew, the Spanish and ours. We'd only stayed out for half that time, and I expected Rhames had offered up reduced rations to the prisoners, as the Spanish had done for us. Checking the barrels and crates, I figured we had three days of water and food.

Should the Caymans prove inhospitable, I had no desire to sail east to Jamaica. Once a pirate haven, the word was out that the British had cleaned out the island. The Mexican coast loomed large and close, but we'd had our share of trouble there as well. That decision could wait, though. The first order of business was to rescue Swift and Red from the cook-pot. Then I would have my revenge on Harp. The Spanish and English would be after him as well, and he knew from my warning about the dangers of the Yucatan with Lafitte's ships on the prowl. The smaller Cayman Islands made sense for him, as well.

It was an uneventful night. Relinquishing the wheel to Mason for the morning watch, I could see the change in him. Rhames was moving about as well, and before I retired, we discussed the weaponry and tactics should we find Harp. The twinkle was back in his eye, but it was clouded. Swift and Red were his brethren and he relished the thought of doing Harp in once we found them, secure in the knowledge that this time I would allow him freedom in his revenge. He and his men would be battle-ready. Leaving the deck, I descended to my cabin, thankfully finding the sewing business over and Shayla asleep on the bunk.

Climbing in next to her, I felt the heat of her body and breathed the smell of her hair. She rolled over and placed an arm over my chest, which I grasped and held tight. Drawing each other close, my sleep was delayed, but when I drifted off, there was surely a smile on my face.

INSTEAD OF SUNLIGHT it was a cool breeze that woke me. It came with the smell of rain through our single open window, the small glass having been removed to make the diving gear. Wondering why I hadn't been notified of a change in the weather, I climbed out of bed and dressed. Shayla cracked an eye open, her smile almost making me return to our bunk, but another gust blew through the open hole.

"Weather." At sea the word needed little expansion.

"A piece of glass would be nice," she said, pulling the frayed blanket around her.

"I'd just as well have Harp's schooner." Aside from the brief conversation on the spar yesterday, we'd spoken little since leaving Havana. From the expression on her face, I could tell she had an eye on revenge as well.

The crew sought blood too, but I knew I had to keep all our emotions in check or we were likely to make a deadly decision.

"We could try and see your father in Grand Cayman," I said, trying to change the subject. Phillip ran a small pub on the large island. He'd helped us salvage the *Ten Sail* wreck, and had left with us, but never found his sea legs.

"Changin' the subject, are you."

"We could marry there. Maybe with the baby, he'd come with us."

"Now there's a thought, but what about the governor?"

It had been two years since we'd been to Grand Cayman. When we'd left, our holds had been full of silver, a lion's share of which the governor thought he was entitled. "Could be there's a new man." It was possible. The Brits didn't fare well in the tropics and often returned to England as soon as their posting ended. If we found and captured Harp, we had another option that might legitimize the entire operation. Handing him over in a British port might result in his ship being awarded to us as a prize.

"Don't think I can't read your mind, Nick Van Doren. Be gone with you."

I was dismissed, but the conversation wasn't over, and I decided to postpone my decision on how to deal with Harp until we actually found him. Leaving Shayla with a kiss on the forehead that soon turned into a passionate embrace. We were almost back in the bunk when a call from the deck forced me to leave her.

The schooner had been spotted.

"We could use you on watch if you're up to it." It was the wrong thing to say, but my mind was focused on Harp.

"Don't you be treating me like an invalid."

Despite the weather the ship was bustling with activity. On my way above, several of Rhames's men crashed into me as they hustled to the gun deck. Stepping aside to allow them to pass, I found myself staring at Rhames.

"Found the bastard."

"Why wasn't I alerted?" Things had gone farther than my liking.

He shrugged, trying to hide his smile. I got the feeling he had delayed long enough to reach the point of no return before I was consulted. "Mason said—"

We were interrupted by a loud boom. My first thought was that we were taking fire, but a flash of lightning brought my attention to the dark skies behind us. Just as I saw it, rain blew in sheets, forcing me to cover my eyes. "And the storm?"

"A blessing from the gods," he said.

Chapter 34

The storm loomed behind us. In front, the three masts of the schooner rose above the low island. From this angle Little Cayman and her sister, Cayman Brac, appeared to be one landmass. The illusion revealed how small they really were—just over twenty miles between them. Harp's ship sat at anchor about a third of the way up Little Cayman. It was a good anchorage for the prevailing winds, but the storm changed those. With the wind at our backs they were now against a lee shore. It would take a skilled captain to keep the ship from grounding. Harp was in no condition to command, and his first mate, who had tried to escape with us, was long forgotten in the Havana prison.

I could see now why Mason and Rhames hadn't bothered to wake me. If not for the storm, Harp would have the upper hand, but with the current conditions we could sail straight towards him, allowing the schooner no chance to maneuver or escape.

A long bolt of lightning lit the sky followed by a crash of thunder. The sound was a distinct crack, not the long rumble of a faraway storm. Looking at the black sky, I realized the squall might cause us more trouble than Harp.

"We'll come straight at 'em." Mason called to the men braving the rain in the rigging to reef the large square-sails. "Rhames'll make the call when to turn."

"I want the boat whole. Red and Swift might still be alive."

He nodded and called for another reef in the sails.

"Right, then." I turned toward the companionway and nearly bumped into Shayla as she approached the mast. "Not today."

"Bugger that. I'm sure-footed as any man."

"But__"

My protest fell on deaf ears. Ignoring my order, she walked past me and started to climb. After a mumbled prayer for her and the baby's safety, I knew that as long as we continued this dangerous lifestyle it didn't matter if she was above or below.

Continuing with my mission, I entered the companionway and found Rhames on the gun deck. "What do you have for shot?"

"Hoping a keg of nails'll do the bastards in."

I was grateful our interests were aligned. As much as we all wanted revenge, rescuing our men and taking the ship were our priorities.

"Right, then." I started to walk away when he called me back.

"What about this old bucket?"

I hadn't thought about the disposition of our present ship. We certainly couldn't leave it with Harp. My intention was to strand him and his crew on the island and head southwest out of these snake-infested waters.

"Load two cannon with six-pounders. Fire what you like for range, no hits, but I want them to feel the splash when the balls hit," I said.

Rhames's smile was back. "Aye. Scare the piss out of the bastards first, then."

"Right, then." I left him with his orders and went back on deck. The crew had assumed their battle stations. An eerie quiet settled over the ship as we waited. Everything was prepared; we just needed to close the gap. Surveying the deck, the grappling hooks were set at intervals of ten feet, each laid on a neatly coiled rope. Boarding the schooner was something few of us besides Rhames had experience with, though the two Scots looked like seasoned veterans. It would be the most dangerous part of the operation.

"How long?" I asked Mason. He stood stoically at the wheel making minor adjustments as we went.

"Should be a minute or two till we make the turn. Which side do you want to shoot from?"

A vessel of our class could only shoot light guns forward or aft. We would need to align ourselves beam to the schooner. The wind had remained steady to the north, making a portside attack the better choice for a fast escape if things went badly. Turning to starboard would put the two islands in our path. I called down to Rhames to prepare his six-pounders for their range shots. An uneasy quiet fell over the deck as each man prepared himself settling in for the wait that was generally worse than the outcome.

"They've spotted us!" came Shayla's voice from above.

I reached for the glass, but before I could bring it to my eye, I saw the schooner hoist the main, in itself a deadly mistake against a lee shore. It was an attempt to escape, but the sizable sail put an enormous strain on the schooner's anchor. It was an act of desperation. Their hope was that the boat would swing before the anchor pulled, allowing them to come about. But if the anchor pulled prematurely they would be driven onto the beach.

"Full speed ahead. Damn the bastards!" I called to

Mason, and ran to the companionway, where I called for Rhames to fire. Seconds later, the ship rocked back as the two test shots flew from the barrels of our guns. Bringing the glass to my eye, I watched them land: One to port and the other just beyond the stern. With the schooner moving forward to retrieve her anchor, I hoped the six-pounders would have the desired effect. The closer to shore the schooner got the less chance she had for an escape. I could only hope there was no coral lurking in the shallow water to break out her bottom.

"Two degrees of elevation and fire another round." I called out the order and went forward to the bowsprit to see the results. Mason knew our plan and cut the wheel hard to starboard, turning the port side to the schooner. Two loud booms followed by a cloud of smoke left us momentarily disoriented. Then the wind cleared the deck, but we had to wait a long minute for the cloud, hanging between us and the schooner, to disperse.

Our ship rolled over the swells and crashed down into the troughs as we sped toward the schooner. Finally, when barely a hundred yards separated the two ships, I could see again. Looking through the glass once more, I watched Harp's crew scurrying around the deck in disarray. He might at one time have been a competent officer, but that no longer applied. In his current state I doubted he could find the head when he needed it.

Pushed forward by our cannon fire, the schooner was up over her anchor. We were close enough I could see the sweat flying off the brows of the crew as they worked the rode around the capstan.

"Get the hooks ready. Fire the next round, Rhames." I called as loud as I could in case to ensure Harp's crew heard. Mason turned to starboard again, and our port cannon unleashed several rounds of nails at the schooner. Once again we had to wait for the smoke to clear before we could see the result.

Whether it was having their backs against the lee shore, the kegs of nails blasted across their decks, or a combination of both, the crew was abandoning ship fast and swimming for shore. Several men were still aboard—one being Harp. Rhames had seen the result of his work and was waiting with a boarding party for my signal.

From the look of her, there would be no resistance. "Find our men. I want Harp alive, and take some of the freedmen to sail her."

I swear Rhames winked at me before climbing over the rail to the waiting skiff. With Harp's crew abandoning ship I decided against the grappling hooks, which would have put us in the same position as the schooner. Trying to save both ships from the entanglement was a fool's errand. Both skiffs were loaded with men, leaving us with a skeleton crew. Knowing we were now exposed to the same kind of attack that we had just executed, I took a nervous look over my shoulder, but saw only water. Though Mason had dropped all our sail, the momentum of the ship carried us toward the schooner and just beyond it, the shore. This business couldn't be over soon enough.

Rhames's skiff had just reached the schooner when I realized that even without sail we were still moving forward at a good rate of speed. The ship was caught in the surf and was itself acting as a sail. Mason noticed it as well, and pulled the wheel hard to starboard, executing our planned exit strategy. We might have won the battle, but were damned close to losing the war if both ships grounded.

A cheer came up from the schooner just as we made our turn. Mason called for the foresails to give him steerage. We had coasted away from the schooner seeking the safety of deeper water when I heard a gunshot. I feared the worst and, glancing at the growing expanse of water between the ships, I knew I had to act now. Hauling my shirt off, I climbed onto the stern rail and dove into the water.

Stroking hard, I found myself going nowhere. Our ship was moving away, but the schooner was no closer. The strong current had ahold of me and it was all I could do to stay in place. It was a dangerous situation, for if I failed, I would be pulled into the depths. The shore to my right was my best chance to escape the deadly current and I devoted all my energy to reaching the shallower water, where the pull would lessen dramatically.

Looking back at the ship, I saw Mason come about, but he likely had no idea of my situation. Once you took your eye off a man overboard, he was forever lost to the sea. Struggling and nearing exhaustion, I noticed the water had lightened and I could see the sandy bottom below. With safety in reach, I stroked harder, finally reaching the depth were the current was insignificant. Recalling the gunshot, there was no time to rest, but without the resistance of the current I quickly reached the schooner and climbed aboard.

Water pooled around me as I stood breathless on deck. Scanning the ship for the cause of the shot, I saw my crew huddled around a figure on the deck. At first I suspected it was Harp, but saw him bound against the mast.

Looking back to the group, I saw who it was.

Chapter 35

STEVEN BECKER
UNCHARTED
Waters

After checking that the demented captain was secured, I called for the Scots to guard him and moved quickly toward the group huddled around the downed man. One of the freedmen moved aside, allowing me to look at Rhames. Though it wasn't always easy, over the years we had grown close. His pirate blood and need to flex his muscles often caused friction and had at one point led him down the path of a mutiny. Our experiences had tempered the bond between us and with all that behind us I trusted him as a brother—a pirate brother.

Blood poured from his shoulder. Remembering how Blue had treated my own gunshot wound, I eased next to him. Clearly in pain, I could see the look of recognition in his eyes, as he tried to speak.

"Make sure that bastard hangs." His eyes went to Harp at the mast.

"Did he shoot you?"

"Bastard surprised me, but we got the ship."

"The men?"

His eyes drifted out of focus as he shook his head. Not sure if it was the pain or the confirmation of the loss of Red and

Swift, I grabbed his shoulders to bring him to the present. A brief survey had been done, and I saw men glance at the pile of bones on deck. This wasn't the time for grief. We would mourn them later.

"Right, then. That was a good piece of work there." Turning to one of the freedmen I asked him to find some rum. Rhames deserved it.

I moved closer, but before I could evaluate the wound a thump jarred us. The keel had hit the bottom. I looked up. We were within a hundred feet of the beach. Between boarding the ship and Rhames's injury, the ship, still powered by the main-sail, had crept beyond her anchor and was in dire straits.

There was no telling how well the hook was set, but I had to assume if the ship had run past it, the hold was precarious. This was evidenced by another thump as the bow brushed against the sand. We needed to get the ship underway. Rhames's injury would have to wait until we had water beneath our keel. Then I would send for Blue and Lucy to take care of him.

"Drop that sail," I ordered, jarring the freedmen into action. The freedmen assumed their assigned posts and the sail was quickly furled, but, as it had done with our ship, the wind continued to push the schooner forward. Racking my mind for a solution, I quickly considered our options. If we had more water beneath us I would drop a drogue to slow our progress, but it was too late for that. The answer came to me as the opposite of what we should do and, as such, I took a minute to think it through and make sure it would work.

Moving back to the helm, I explained my plan to the freedman at the wheel. His expression betrayed his suspicions, but he did as I asked and called for the foresails. The only way out of this mess was to make enough headway to come about. With our bow already brushing bottom that meant we would have to pull her back on her anchor and kedge her backwards.

I could only hope as I led the rest of the crew to the capstan that the anchor would hold.

The wheel seemed frozen as the anchor rode fought the forward progress of the ship. I knew once the anchor broke free we would have enough speed to come about, but a ship this size needed room to turn, and the slim piece of water between us and the beach looked narrower by the second. Finally, between gusts, the wheel moved. Driving with my legs, I pushed hard against the capstan while encouraging the others to do the same. Chain started to come in and at first we seemed to be treading water, but I soon noticed the shore was just a bit farther away.

As we gained momentum the rode came up with less effort and we were soon above the anchor. It was time to see if the gamble would pay off.

"Ready at the helm!" I yelled toward the steersman. Without waiting for an acknowledgment, I urged the men for one final push around the capstan. The resistance seemed like it would never end, but finally the anchor broke free, landing us in a pile on the deck. As I ran to the helm I again yelled to the men to finish retrieving the anchor. With the mechanical advantage provided by the capstan it was easy work and I could hear the chain rattling around the block as I moved to the wheel.

The steersman had felt it too and spun the wheel hard to starboard. The foresails dumped the wind as we turned, leaving our only power the forward momentum we had built. At first I thought it wasn't going to be enough, but the bow kept turning and soon faced open water. Glancing back at the beach I saw we had cleared it by less than fifty feet.

A cheer went up as we swung the ninety degrees necessary to complete the maneuver. Before the sails filled the men knew the maneuver was successful. Slowly we started moving away from the island. Glancing back at Rhames, I saw the old bugger leaning against a barrel with a bottle in his hand and a twisted grimace on his face. He would live.

Next we had to rendezvous with our ship, and scanning the horizon I found her about a quarter-mile out. The freedman adjusted our course, and I went to Rhames and assured him that help was on the way, then crossed the deck and stood over Harp.

There were few men I had come across against whom I held a grudge —few that still lived—and the mutinous British captain was one of them. Kicking his leg, I glared down at him.

"It'll be the gallows for you."

He turned to look at me and I could see the evidence of the beating my men had given him after he'd shot Rhames. Ordinarily I would have punished them for it, but in this case, it was well-deserved.

Spitting out blood, he tried to say something. A tooth came out as he spat again and I backed away slightly.

"You think it's that easy, do you? I'm a British officer."

"Was."

"What do you intend?"

"We'll let the governor on Grand Cayman decide your fate."

He lowered his head in what looked like defeat, but knowing the man I was sure he wasn't finished. As if to signal our victory, sunlight broke through and I realized I hadn't noticed the storm clear out. With the wind down the two ships were soon rafted side-by-side, and I climbed over the rail to our old ship, sending Lucy and Blue to help Rhames the moment my feet landed on deck. Once they had passed over, I walked to the binnacle, where Mason stood in the same stoic position where I had left him several hours earlier.

"Well, you've got yourself a new ship," I greeted him.

"She ought to do once we wipe Harp's stink from her." He paused. "We don't have the men to sail both ships."

As for what was now our old ship, I agreed. We could easily leave it here with enough provisions for the British crew to sail to a friendly port. They shouldn't have much trouble pleading their innocence with Harp in irons.

"Right, then. Strip her of weapons and we'll leave it for Harp's crew. They'll not suffer by my hand for their captain's madness."

Mason nodded and called one of the freedmen over. He allowed the larger guns to be left in place, but the smaller cannonades, shot, and powder would all be removed. The man nodded and left us.

"What about him?" Mason asked, jerking his head in the direction of Harp, who was being escorted across a plank set between the two ships.

"We'll drop him by Grand Cayman and let the governor deal with him. I was hoping that by showing a little good faith, we might be allowed to spend some of our gold."

"Let's hope we get a friendlier welcome than last time."

"There might be a new man now. Without Pott, the old one had no chance. " Pott had been the governor's aid when we were here last. Assigned to us to keep track of the treasure recovered, he had ended up wanting to stay aboard, then found a home in Great Inagua, where we had installed him in place of the magistrate there.

"You might want to send a few men to find out for sure before you get all bold and set foot on British soil."

It was a good idea, but Mason was the only one I trusted to go ashore without causing an incident. The freedmen were just that. They would have access to some areas in the city, but not others. Sending Rhames or the Scots would surely result in trouble.

"Right, then. You and Shayla will go ashore. I promised

she could see her father and she knows the island. Have two freedmen you can trust row you over and let them see what they can find out as well."

We would wait out the night offshore of Little Cayman and cross the sixty-odd miles of open water to Grand Cayman in the morning. With the exception of the east end, where we had salvaged the *Ten Sail,* most of the large island had deep water right up to her beaches. We would find a quiet anchorage in the lee of one and see what the next day brought.

Chapter 36

STEVEN BECKER

UNCHARTED *Waters*

Watching Shayla being rowed toward shore brought a sense of urgency to the situation. Though she had grown up here, there was no telling what the political climate was and her life could well be in danger. Mason with his level head could avoid trouble and would do what he could to protect her, but he was not a fighter.

Turning away, knowing there was nothing I could do until she returned, I decided to inventory the schooner. After a discussion last night, we had decided to flaunt the sea gods' wrath and change the ship's name from *Baracouta* to *Dorado*. Superstition said it was bad luck to change a ship's name, but in this case, we felt it warranted.

The *Dorado* was newer than any ship I had been on, and it showed in the fitting. Rather than pace the deck I decided to check the rigging. Finding myself on the top spar I chanced another glance at shore. There was no sign of the skiff. It must have passed the low headland that blocked our view of the harbor, and also served to obscure us from their watchmen. Turning my attention back to the sails and rigging, I inspected all three masts before moving down to the deck. Everything appeared to be in order, in what the Brits called "Bristol fashion." Harp might have lost his mind and turned to piracy, but the ship, except for the clutter on deck, didn't reflect it. With our small group gathered, we said a prayer for Red and Swift, following which the cook pot had been dumped into the water.

The holds showed no surprises. We would indeed need to provision, but I estimated there was a week's worth of rations and fresh water aboard. Add to that the fish that Blue and Lucy were sure to catch enroute, and we had enough to make it across to Central America. If relations with the government here proved fruitful, I had no problem leaving some gold behind for the security of a full larder. From here we would be moving into uncharted waters and after our past encounters with natives and pirates, a fully provisioned ship would be to our advantage.

Moving down to the gun deck, I ran into MacDuggal.

"No wonder they didn't fight back. Godawful setup they have here," he said.

"And Rhames?"

"Lucy, God bless her, has him fixed up pretty well. Won't be worth much with a cutlass for a bit, but his spirit's still there."

With the refitting of the deck well in hand, the crew was in the process of dismantling the smaller guns, which would be remounted fore and aft on deck, giving the remaining dozen guns more maneuverability. Men grunted under the strain of the block and tackle required to shift the guns.

"What about shot and powder?"

"Aye. He was low, but with our stores brought aboard, we've got enough for a few battles."

"Small arms?"

"We'll be getting to them in a bit."

I asked the Scotsman to update me with a list of supplies, and dropped down to the next level. The primary function of the ship was trade. She had enough armaments to protect her, but she was a built to transport goods. With deep holds, reaching down three levels from the access hatches on deck, she could handle a load and then some. I'd had the hatches removed to provide more light, and the sun caught the golden bars we had moved from our own hold. In the large space the piles of bars looked small. Counting the bars was short work. Our treasure was seriously diminished by the Spanish captain, but we had Shayla and Lucy back, as well as our freedom. To the side of the bars was our dive gear and pumps. The second skiff was also broken down and stored there.

After stripping Lafitte's ship we had left it at anchor, close enough to the beach for Harp's crew to escape the island. Light on ballast, short the two pumps we had converted for diving, and stripped of light guns, shot, and powder, she would limp into whatever port her men found.

Leaving the forward hold, I moved aft to inspect the rear hold. It too was almost bare. Harp's madness had affected his decisions, and his pirate career had been a failure. The pumps and bilge were what I expected for a newer ship. Everything appeared to be in working order and I climbed back to the main deck to check on Rhames.

I found him lying on a coil of rope. With Blue and Lucy hovering over him, he had a piece of Blue's bark in one hand and a bottle in the other. Normally, alcohol was rationed, something I would have to enforce now that we had found several kegs of rum aboard. I let him be, understanding his pain. The wound from my own gunshot was healing well, but I still felt it, especially at night.

"Ought to have some word from shore pretty soon."

"Aye." He took a swig from his bottle, and stuffed the bark back in his mouth. "The Scots have things in hand?"

"Looks to be alright, but if you're up and about soon, I'd

appreciate you having a look." I wanted to confirm Rhames's authority.

"Aye, between the rum and this stuff," he said, pulling the bark from his mouth, "I'm ready for action."

I was well aware of the medicinal powers of the bark, but wanted to see his condition first hand. Between taking several bullets and the panther attack in the Florida Everglades, I was accustomed to the healing process. Pulling back the cloth covering his shoulder, I checked the wound. It was a mild pink, not bright red or dull green, signs that things were about to turn bad. Just as I replaced the bandage I heard a call from the lookout.

"Skiff!"

Leaving Rhames, I ran to the opposite rail and with my hand to my brow, scanned the water. A boat was indeed coming toward us, but was too far away to make out the occupants. Running to the binnacle, I grabbed the glass and returned to the rail. Focusing on the small boat, I counted heads. Four had left, but five were returning. The figures were still too far away to identify, but a surge of relief swept through me when I saw that one was a woman.

The minutes passed slowly until the skiff reached the ship.

"Phillip!" I called down to the fifth man.

"Nick."

I was glad to see him. We had gotten on well during our time together; it was the sea that he didn't get along with. The skiff bumped against the ship and one of the freedmen reached for the rope ladder. Shayla was first up, followed by Phillip, Mason, and the freedmen, the last of whom secured the skiff with a painter.

"Good to see you, old man," I greeted Phillip warmly.

"By God, you're still alive. I'm grateful for you taking care of my girl here." He squeezed Shayla's shoulders.

If he only knew what his girl had been through over the

past few adventures his tone might have changed. A wink from Shayla confirmed that she had told him little.

"Right, then. What's the state of affairs on the island?"

"You were right. The old governor was recalled just after our incident. The new man's supposed to be fair," Shayla said.

Phillip confirmed her statement.

"Any danger in me taking Harp in?"

"I'd think he'd be grateful," Phillip said.

Mason was shaking his head behind them. The sun was starting to drop toward the horizon. It was too late for another trip to shore, leaving me the night to make a decision. I would talk to Mason privately to see what was bothering him. With a quick glance over her shoulder showing a smile, Shayla took Phillip by the hand and led him to the companionway to show him his cabin. I wasn't sure if he was with us for the duration or the night, but I wanted him comfortable. Fortunately, the ship had several more private berths than Lafitte's old ship, giving us plenty of room.

I watched until they disappeared, then moved to the helm to find Mason.

"What did you see?"

"Talked to the men working the pier while Shayla went after her father."

I had not wanted him to leave her alone, but that water was under the bridge. "And?"

"There wasn't no talk of Harp or British pirates. I brought up his name in conversation, but got nothing but vacant looks. It's my feeling they don't know he's turned."

"And if I bring him to the governor, it's likely to turn on me?"

"That's what I'm seeing. I'd drop that bastard on the pier and clear out of these waters. The Brits always take care of their own. Without a warrant for him, I wouldn't expect this to be any different."

"Right, then. Make ready to sail tonight. I'll get the Scots to handle this." The two men had fit right in, but trusting them with Harp was a risk. They'd never met Red or Swift, and as a result, I expected they might be more rational, and I decided to test them. I was past worrying how it would turn out, so long as he was off the ship and we were over the horizon before anyone tried to figure out who was lying. In any event, his disease was sure to progress, taking him from madness to death. The knowledge he would suffer, as Red, Swift, and who knew how many others had, was revenge enough for me. In the grand scheme of things dumping Harp and leaving the island were pretty insignificant. The expressions on the faces of the crew as we gathered along the rail, watching Harp being rowed to shore went from happy to see him go to angry that he hadn't been dealt justice aboard—in the pirate way.

Chapter 37

STEVEN BECKER

UNCHARTED
Waters

"Skiff coming."

It was Shayla's voice from the spar that halted the activity on deck. Leaving Mason to complete the preparations for our departure, I scaled the rigging and stood next to her. She handed me the glass, which I focused on the boat coming toward us. From the conspiratorial looks between the Scots and Rhames earlier, I wondered if it had been a mistake to trust the errand to them. Their orders had been to drop off a bound Harp, leaving him at the pier with instructions to alert the magistrate. I now wondered if he had been alive when they left him.

We had made haste for our departure, but apparently something was amiss. The Caribbean generally ran at a slow pace, and it surprised me a reaction had occurred so quickly. Being unexpected, I naturally presumed it was bad news and scanned the deck to see if we could leave before the skiff reached us. The Cayman's were the western extent of the British holdings, and I doubted we needed their good will any longer. But after judging the distance and our state of readiness, it appeared we would have at the least a conversation.

Climbing back down, I found the deck awash in activity. Rhames was up and about, his arm in a sling and a piece of Blue's bark in his mouth. He had seen the skiff as well and sought me out.

"Blow the bastards from the water's what I'd do."

He was still upset about being the only casualty on our raid to take the schooner. "I'll go as far as training a few guns on them—just in case." That seemed to appease him and I watched as he quickly disappeared through the companionway.

"Might as well be courteous. But small arms are in order," I told MacDuggal, who was standing in front of the open armory. He handed me a pistol and took another for himself. Checking mine, I was glad when I saw a light sheen of oil keeping the rust at bay. MacDonald handed me several bullets and a kit to load the gun. Shoving the pistol in my belt, I went toward the binnacle where Mason was directing the crew.

"How long?"

"Another fifteen minutes and we'll be pulling the hook."

Checking the progress of the approaching skiff, there was no question it would arrive before we were ready. A closer inspection revealed several uniformed men at the oars and an officer giving direction. In the bow, with a scowl etched on his face, was a well-dressed man.

"Ahoy!"

"Come aboard if you wish," I called back, signaling the two freedmen by me to lower the rope ladder. The men at the oars easily maneuvered the small craft against the side of the schooner and secured her painter. The officer and the other man started to climb the ladder. I'd seen no weapons other than the officer's sword, which was more decoration than dangerous, and relaxed slightly as he climbed over the rail. The other man followed and we stood staring at each other.

"Nick!" Shayla called down.

I looked up and saw her pointing at the harbor entrance, where the bowsprit of a frigate appeared. It was a warship. I cursed under my breath that we had taken our time departing.

"Nick Van Doren," I said, extending my hand to the man.

"Governor Beekham." He took the offered hand.

"Can I offer you anything?"

"No, we're not here to exchange pleasantries."

I was about to ask what they were here for when he continued.

"That man you dropped. He is a British officer."

"He's nothing but a deranged pirate. Send word to Havana that you have him and you'll get the story."

"The Spanish?" He spat on the deck, as if talking to them repulsed him.

I rattled off what I knew of Harp and his exploits. He remained unfazed, not surprising, as the British were notorious for taking care of their own.

"He has a different story."

"Of course he does." I was getting frustrated, thinking I should have listened to Rhames and dropped Harp, wrapped in chains, to the ocean floor.

"We left a ship for his men. They should be coming this way before too long. They'll vouch for me."

"They've already landed on the other coast. They seem to think you have a treasure aboard."

It always came down to gold. With the frigate quickly approaching, there was little choice but to tell the truth. "We salvage wrecks and such." I remembered the gold lying undis-guised in the hold. "We've got some gold from a job in Haiti."

"Ah, and what flag were you flying at the time?"

He knew more than he should, and I wondered how he got his information. Haiti's close proximity to the Bahamas had us flying the Union Jack. "We're independent." It sounded as hollow as it was.

"Hmm. American by the sound of you."

"Dutch, actually." Our conversation was doing little beside letting the frigate close the gap between us, which may have been his intent. Looking at Beekham, I wondered if he was in fact the governor or a decoy. As I studied his face, I saw a hint of fear, as if he was not accustomed to this game. The other officer carried himself like one, but his rank could be exaggerated as well. Now that I had sniffed out their ruse, I had the upper hand.

"You'll disembark to the frigate and stand trial as pirates." His voice wavered slightly, confirming my guess.

"And why would we do that?" I moved my right hand behind my back and made a slashing gesture. If Mason or Rhames saw it, they would understand.

They both had, and as I started to negotiate terms, I saw Rhames disappear into the companionway and Mason move to the wheel. A minute later, I felt the schooner shift as the gun ports opened and the starboard-side guns were winched forward to their firing positions. One of the foresails was unfurled at the same time and the ship swung on the anchor.

"What is your intention, Captain?" the officer asked, frantically looking back and forth. He knew what we were up to and was helpless to stop us.

"If I wanted to see my wife tonight, I might drop down to that skiff of yours and clear out, Governor," the title heavy with sarcasm. The officer stood stoically evaluating the situation, but beads of sweat appeared on both men's brows.

"Rhames!" I called when the frigate was in easy range. Though she presented a narrow profile with her bow facing toward to us, she was also defenseless until she was able to turn, something I would not allow. The two Brits standing in front of me were clearly sacrificial lambs and the frigate's captain would shoot regardless of them being aboard.

"Fire!"

The ship rocked back, and within seconds of each other, the cannons let loose their charges. The wind had picked up and the smoke quickly moved downwind, just in time for me to see the two British imposters climb the rail and drop down the rope ladder.

"Weigh anchor," I called to Mason, and headed to the capstan to help.

Sails snapped as they caught the wind, and with six men on the capstan, the anchor easily broke free. The schooner moved forward and within a few minutes was plowing through the seas. I hadn't taken the time to see what damage we had inflicted on the frigate. Sinking it was not a priority; escape was. A charge of piracy was enough for a trip to the gallows; I didn't need a murder charge added to make it easier.

On a beam reach and heading due south, the island quickly dropped behind us. Shayla was still aloft and I called up to ask if she saw pursuit. When her answer came back negative I relaxed slightly. We had burnt another bridge, but were still alive to tell of it. Once again trying to do the right thing had cost us, a lesson that left a bad taste in my mouth. As we moved south the ship quickly settled into her normal routine as the Caymans dropped below the horizon. The best we could do was to put as much water between us and our enemies as we could, and with the *Dorado* that was easily accomplished.

Shayla dropped to the deck and reached for my hand. "Not the outcome we expected, but I'm glad we stopped."

"Phillip alright?" We had been too busy to see if he intended to leave his home and travel with us. In any event, his decision had been made for him, and seeing the smile on Shayla's face I was glad he was aboard.

Before she could answer Blue came running toward me. "Rhames. The bastard's down."

Without a word, we followed him to the companionway and down to the gun deck. Rhames was propped up against a post with Lucy and the Scots hovering over him. Moving toward him, there was no sign of our victory on his face—only pain.

Chapter 38

"He needs more powerful medicine than I have," Lucy said.

I looked down at Rhames. Unable to stay out of the action, he had tried to help the men and opened the wound, which now saturated his blouse with blood.

"Get Shayla and Phillip," I called to one of the freedmen.

Rhames looked pale, maybe from losing so much blood, maybe from the lead lodged deep in his shoulder.

"Some rum if you would?" he asked.

"You're lucky we've got these two and not some sawbones who would have your arm."

"Don't I know it. Got hit by the backlash from one of the guns."

It didn't surprise me that he was so close to the action. I probably would have done the same. Now, as Lucy pulled the fabric away I knew right away that the wound would need to be cauterized. If it were smaller, it would be a simple matter of sealing it with a red-hot iron, but the open flesh was inches in diameter.

Shayla and Phillip came beside me.

"It's bad. We've got to burn it," Shayla said.

"I'll be needin' that rum now," Rhames said.

"You'll be needing more than that." I'd had red-hot steel put to me before, although to a smaller area. This would be unbearable. Sending a man for the rum, I asked several others to hold him down. Lucy and Shayla had a pile of black powder and a match ready, but Rhames waved them off until his rum arrived. When it did, he drank deeply from the bottle before Shayla grabbed it from him and poured a generous amount into the open wound.

Rhames screamed and bucked the men holding him down, but his strength quickly failed. Lucy wasted no time and packed the wound with black powder.

"Give him something in his mouth," she said, as she prepared to light the powder.

I yanked my belt free, folded it, and placed it between Rhames's teeth, but not before he'd had another mouthful of rum. Our eyes met and I saw his pain. There was nothing to do now except get it done. Lucy struck the match and lit the powder. We jumped back as one when it ignited, but the men held firm to Rhames, who appeared to have fainted. I would ask the men to keep that part to themselves in order to preserve his dignity.

The smell of burnt flesh in the confines of the gun deck soon overtook us. It was soon only Shayla, Blue, Lucy, and I attending the old pirate. Finally, his eyes cracked and he forced them open.

He spat out the belt. "Not as bad as I expected," he said through gritted teeth.

Knowing that he was alright, for now, I left him. The smell of the sea was a welcome relief to the carnage, and I drank it in before heading to the helm. Unaware of what was happening below, Mason lightly gripped the spokes of the wheel as he guided the schooner south, wearing a rare smile on his weathered face.

"She sails well."

Coming from Mason, that was a compliment of the highest order. "Learn her secrets."

"We'll be as tight as a nun's privates before long." His face tightened and the smile disappeared. "Heard about Rhames."

"He'll be alright, but he's seen his last fight," I said.

"That'll be the end of him."

"He's strong." Rhames would need every bit of his constitution to find his place now that his arm would likely be useless. Men did come back from injuries, but Rhames's position was garnered from his ability to fight.

Mason knew it, too, and changed the subject. "Not likely we'll run out of water, but we'll be needing a destination before long."

The *Dorado* opened up a new world for us. Among the fastest ships in the sea, she was able to sail within a few degrees of the wind, not restricted to only a few points of sail like the older ships. In addition to her maneuverability and speed, she was built for weather. Rounding the Horn, with the area's notorious wind and seas that could change almost instantly, we would stand a chance—unlike Lafitte's ship, which would have been gambling with the devil. With several thousand miles ahead of us to get a feel for the schooner, by the time we reached the Cape, we would be ready for the crossing into the Pacific.

I looked down at the chart to an area that once had been the destination of my family. Seven-hundred-fifty miles to the southeast lay a small group of islands still under Dutch rule. They were the closest chance of a friendly port. Doing a quick calculation, I expected we could make landfall in a week. But the journey would take us to the limit of our provisions.

"These islands here." I pointed to the small group off the northern tip of South America.

"The Netherland Antilles. Hoping they'll be friendly to us, are you?"

"Counting on it." The trade route followed the curve of the Windward Islands further to the east. I expected there would be little traffic in this destitute area of the Caribbean and therefore we would arrive just north of the equator unde-tected. Once we crossed the line, there was even less of a chance we would be recognized.

Mason appeared satisfied with my choice and was soon lost in his charts. Taking my leave, I went by to check on Rhames. Propped up against a coil of rope with a bottle in his hand and the piece of bark dangling between his lips, he was sound asleep.

A strange feeling of complacency came over me. After being on the run for the better part of three years, I finally felt free. The exhaustion I had been carrying with me fell away, and as I crossed into the companionway I felt the first wave of fatigue. Reaching the cabin, I found it empty, and without another thought I collapsed onto our bunk and was quickly asleep.

When I finally woke, I found myself alone in the bunk. I vaguely recalled Shayla coming to bed sometime in the night and, as the sun was above our porthole, I expected she had already risen. My body seemed to resist movement as I rose, but once on my feet I felt refreshed. Washing from a bucket of tepid water left on the sideboard, I changed into clean clothes and went on deck.

A ship at sea quickly falls into a routine. Some thrive off it, but for me, boredom quickly sets in. Unless we were in danger, I rarely took a watch, but occupied myself with projects, some that needed doing, and others that were mere whims. Blue was often my accomplice in this, and it was on an inspection of the bilge and pumps that we found the first sign of trouble.

The bilge was as dry as I had seen aboard a ship, but two

of the four pumps were out of service. Fortunately, there were ample spare parts to bring them back into working order, but it showed me that despite the newness of the vessel, every ship has problems. As we continued our inspection I became ever more vigilant, as we found numerous small areas that needed maintenance. By the time we reached the deck several hours later, I had a list that would take several men the better part of the trip to complete.

We ate a meal of dried biscuits accompanied by weak wine. I had decided to save Harp's good rum for Rhames, so the rest of us suffered with the crew's rations. With Blue and Lucy aboard, our table fare was often complemented with fresh fish, and the two of them spent the next afternoon hauling several large dorado and tuna over the rail. That night's meal, though the wine was the same, was quite a bit more palatable.

The days passed quickly, and nearing the end of the week, the ship was prepared for whatever faced her. Rhames had recovered enough to take short walks around the deck, and we had a hard talk about his condition. Reducing his rum ration did not go well, but there was still an ample supply of the bark, which kept him happy in the short term. The men treated him like a hero, and for the time being he would be alright. As we approached land I encouraged him to drill his crews and service the weapons. With his cutlass shifted to his left side, he used it as a pointer as he directed the men.

Shayla and Phillip had spent a few days catching up, but they soon drifted into their own patterns. Shayla, obsessed with anything to do with the baby, was making a variety of clothes, while Phillip took what materials he could find and started to fashion a crib. His skill had caught my attention.

I found Phillip in the small workshop below, where he was driving dowels into two long pieces of wood. We'd been without a carpenter for months now, and it was evident in some of our makeshift repairs.

"It's coming along nicely," I said, rubbing my hand across the well-sanded wood. "I'm hoping you're happy to be here. Shayla certainly is."

"Seeing as there was little choice, I am." He looked up and winked. "Truth be told, I've missed Shayla and now with the baby and all, I'm grateful to be here."

"From the look of things, you could fill in as carpenter, if you'll have the job."

"Got to stay busy. Not much need for a pub-keeper on a ship, is there now?"

We worked out the terms and his share, and on leaving I was glad to have him, as both the ship's new carpenter and my future father-in-law.

I was about to turn back and have a last look at the crib when I heard the call of "Land ho!" from the deck.

Chapter 39

STEVEN BECKER

UNCHARTED
Waters

The similarities between the island that lay on the horizon and Grand Cayman were so great that if we hadn't been at sea a week I would have thought we had remained at anchor. As we approached, it appeared more brown than Grand Cayman, but from this distance that could be an illusion. With no local knowledge, Mason had two men dropping wax-bottomed leads from the bowsprit and one man running a log-line from amidships.

The calls came back "no bottom" until we were within a hundred yards of the beach, when the first lead hit.

"Sand at five fathoms," the man called, after checking what material the wax had attracted to the bottom of the weight.

As we approached what looked like a small inlet, Mason dropped most of our sail, leaving only the foresails. With our speed checked, the calls came back indicating a gradual rise to the bottom. Finally, within a hundred yards of a white-sand beach we dropped anchor. Once the sails were lashed and the deck put into order, the crew clamored at the rail for a chance to go ashore.

Rhames pushed through the group, his swagger as big as

ever. "Out of the way, ya bastards. We'll have a group scout the beach right quick. Then you can all dip your toes in the sand."

Feeling Shayla beside me, I too, fought the urge to walk on land. It had been an easy trip, but after a week aboard of eating fish and dry biscuits, we hoped for at least fresh water and hunting. For my part, I had been practicing my rusty Dutch, hoping to find some compatriots amongst the inhabitants.

The beach remained quiet and the first party ashore came back with no sightings of either game or people. Evaluating our position, I climbed into the rigging to see if there was a better view to be had. Standing on the top spar, I scanned first the surrounding water, and seeing no ships, turned my attention inland. The island was like nothing I had seen. If I thought Great Inagua a dry island, this was several steps closer to hell. Cactus dotted the landscape. We'd seen the plants before, but they were abundant here. The trees, mere scrubs, were surrounded by every shape of prickly plant you could imagine. Heat waves shimmered from the arid soil, making it seem even drier. What I didn't see was any sign of man.

"We'll need two expeditions in the morning," I told Rhames and Mason. "One to check out the interior. The other can take the skiff and circumnavigate the island. According to the chart, there's a settlement of some sort on the other side." The mood had turned slightly sour after seeing the inhospitable island. While we were accustomed to wild boar, the only game here appeared to be large iguanas.

"Seems like your countrymen got pushed into a corner here."

It appeared so. Something in the way he said it brought back my heritage and with the memory came the name Moses Cohen Henriques. The early days of discovery were a hard time for the Jews on the Iberian Peninsula.

Faced with the Inquisition in Spain, many Jews had turned

into *Conversos*, at least on the surface, adopting the Christian faith. This ploy was effective until the Spanish monarchs decided to rid their country of Jews altogether. Many migrated to the Americas. The new continents were far enough from the seat of power to no longer care, and the Jews thrived as traders for several decades until the Inquisitors followed them to the New World.

Henriques was one of those men forced to leave Spain. Many chose to fit in the best they could, but the Sephardi had rebelled, turned pirate, and taken the entire 1628 Plate Fleet. Other pirates were more notorious, but Henriques's prize was the biggest ever taken. We had found a small cache from it stashed in a cave on Cozumel.

After taking his prize, Henriques lived on an island off the coast of Brazil, but his notoriety made him a target of the Inquisitors, forcing him to flee. His life and the disposition of the treasure are undocumented after that, except for a close group of Sephardi who passed the secret from generation to generation. Emanuel, the turncoat who had blown up the *Panther*, was one, and he had told me the pirate's story. He knew Henriques had stashed a part of his wealth on Cozumel and, unable to find it himself, he had used us, then tried to kill us.

Knowing our reserves were dwindling after I had paid off the Spanish captain for Shayla and Lucy's release, I doubted we had enough gold to see us around the Horn and to a new life. Though the island was initially disappointing, I still held out hope. The Dutch had been hospitable to the homeless Jews. Recognizing their ability as traders and merchants, they had been accepted in Amsterdam, where my family hailed from. It was my guess that somewhere in the Antilles, someone knew where the rest of the Henriques's treasure was.

The boredom and rest that accompanied with our journey quickly turned to anxiety and restlessness. Knowing I was so close to my own people, but unsure how well I would be accepted, wore heavily on me. Shayla noticed it and tried to calm me, but I had a feeling deep within that if we were not accepted here, we might never find a home.

Finally the night turned into day, and after seeing the shore party off, I set out in the skiff with three of the freedmen to see if we could find a settlement. Having four of us allowed shifts at the oars, of which I would take my fair share. From the look of the island on the chart, it would be a twenty-mile row around to the city. Not knowing what our reception would be like, we chose to keep the *Dorado* anchored here, and with strong backs pulling the oars, we left eager to see what lay on the other side. Setting off into the rising sun, we rounded the eastern point, and still finding nothing of interest, continued around. The monotonous shoreline crept by as we rowed, until we came upon what looked to be a deep-water anchorage.

I saw faint tendrils of smoke rising to the west. We rowed past another point and I saw the source. A town appeared. Still not knowing how well we would be received, I scanned the harbor as if it were an enemy port. Several brigs were anchored close to shore, but there was no military presence. A long, narrow wharf extended a couple of hundred feet spanning an area of brown shallows to the deep-blue water. Pointing it out to the men on the oars, we started for it.

The water was indeed deep enough to allow a full-sized ship to dock. Though it was empty, we rowed around the end, where I secured the painter to one of the piers and, leaving two of the freedmen to watch the skiff, the other, Luis, disembarked with me. Starting down the dock, I saw several men coming toward me.

Not wanting to appear threatening, we halted and waited for them to approach. I wiped my sweaty hands on my britches several times before they reached us and was about to do it again when the first man extended his hand in a warm greeting. I bade him good day in Dutch, which made him smile.

"And to you, sir. Might we ask who you are and whence you came?"

"Nick Van Doren, at your service," I said, bowing slightly. I introduced Luis and waited to make their acquaintance.

"This here's Hendrik, and I'm Abraham."

"We have a ship anchored on the other side of the island. Hoping we could provision here. We're headed around the Horn."

"That's a fair ways. Your name? I knew a Van Doren in Amsterdam."

I started our story, and just as I mentioned being taken by pirates, he stopped me.

"Your father's name?"

"Hans."

He bowed his head slightly and without letting me continue, led us down the dock and into a small building that I guessed to be a customs house. After offering weak beer, he asked me to continue. Both men listened attentively as I told the story of being taken by Gasparilla and our subsequent adventures. Deciding to let them draw their own conclusions, I was truthful in all regards, except my omission of the word *pirate*. When I finished the story, he leaned forward.

"I think I knew your pa."

My heart leapt, but I tried to calm down when Abraham excused himself.

"Could be another, of course, but not too many Hans Van Doren's came across in '21. We wondered what came of your family. Any idea what happened to them?"

I told him that I feared the worst and he looked at the floor, shaking this head.

Finally Henrik spoke. "You and your crew are welcome

here. I'll send word to your men to bring your ship around. You can anchor here and provision."

I felt I could trust them, but after all we'd been through, I thought it better that I brought the ship.

"I certainly appreciate your hospitality, but it's better if I went back."

"That won't be necessary." Abraham had returned with three armed men. "Send them word. You'll be fairly treated until they arrive." He thrust a piece of parchment and quill toward me.

Chapter 40

I wasn't sure if I was under arrest, or a guest, but either way, it was far from the reception I expected. Fortunately, I still remembered enough Dutch to understand what was being said. Abraham remained with me while Hendrik went to assemble what I assumed was their governing council. Gasparilla had educated me in political dealing, and over the last few years I liked to think my diplomatic skills had improved. As it turned out, bloodshed and violence were all-too-key components of negotiation.

The Spanish were pompous characters who needed to be coddled. The English were all about protocol. I had yet to determine what made the Dutch tick, but as I remembered from my father, it was probably profit. The Dutch East and West India companies had more to do with ruling their colonies than the actual government did. That led me to believe that my "captivity" had something to do with money. In any case, that was better than the pirate label we often carried. While the men assembled, I did my best to take in snippets of what conversations I could understand.

After an hour of waiting, six men sat at the table facing me.

The Caribbean climate was not suitable for many northern Europeans, and these men were no different. Flushed faces and heavy girths were the norm among the men, who wiped their brows with handkerchiefs as they sat.

"Van Doren, is it?"

"Right. Nick Van Doren."

"And your father was Hans?"

"Yes, but there could be more than one." The looks from the men were dismissive when I suggested it. A brief silence prevailed while they mopped their brows.

"There is the matter of a debt that Hans Van Doren owes to the Dutch West India Company, who we represent. Seems he was a bit of a speculator."

My guess that this was somehow about money was correct. "My father's debts, if he had any, don't concern me. I was twelve at the time we were taken by Gasparilla. I know nothing of this *speculating*." I said it dismissively, as if it didn't concern me, but from their expressions, it did.

"Seems like the apple doesn't fall far from the tree, eh. A bit of bad luck, I'd say," Henrik said. "But, a debt is a debt and now that you are here, we must address it."

I had seen no ships capable of pursuing us if we chose to escape, but there was the matter of provisions. "What would be the size of the debt, then?"

One of the men cleared his throat. "Ten thousand guilders, give or take."

"Give or take?" I expected a better accounting if I were to be responsible. "And how was this debt incurred?"

"Your father was a shrewd man, but he had dreams of finding treasure. Apparently he had a theory and borrowed the money to bring his family to America."

I didn't know if I should be happy or sad that I was following in my father's footsteps. "We were taken by pirates."

"And now, some might say you are one," one of the men said.

There was more brow-mopping and throat-clearing before Hendrik, who appeared to be their leader, spoke. "We've heard of your exploits reclaiming treasure from the sea. Perhaps there is a way to repay your family's debt."

Now we were getting to the heart of it. I waited for the details.

"Your father had compelling evidence about the location of a treasure."

This was starting to sound familiar. I nodded and let him continue.

"The Dutch were accommodating to the Jews forced from Spain during the Inquisition. Many were able seamen and traders, all needed in the New World. Under the seal of the Netherlands, letters of marque were issued to some, and in exchange for the protection of our government, the captains were free to pursue the Spanish treasure galleons. Many prospered, and the Spanish were crippled by their actions, but the sea takes its own share."

I wasn't sure if I should be excited or worried.

"We would propose a joint venture of sorts to recover one of the largest."

"Moses Cohen Henriques, then?"

They set their handkerchiefs down and stared at me.

"You know of him?"

I explained our meeting Emanuel in Cozumel and finding the cache in the cenote, then the double-cross that had blown up our ship in the harbor there. I left their imaginations to the fate of the treasure.

"Fleeing the inquisitors in Brazil, and with his Sephardic roots, he originally sought safe haven here. Our predecessors granted his petition, but the Spanish found him before he could reach Curacao. From what we have gathered, one of his ships escaped and reached Mexico."

Their story rang true. "And the location of the wreck?"

"That'll require that we have a deal first," Hendrik said.

The others' heads bobbed up in down in unison. "I can't very well start a negotiation without knowing what we are up against." Escape was starting to sound like the best option.

Hendrik mopped his brow again. "Enough to say it is near shore."

"How deep would the water be?"

"No more than ten fathoms."

That was the outer limit of what we had dived, but if the water was protected, with the new gear we could do it. "And what do you have in mind, then?"

"We'll need a surety, of course." It was Abraham who spoke.

"And what if we have nothing to give?" They were confident that we had, and I wondered where they had gotten their information.

"The West India Company has a wide reach."

That was as much of an answer as I was going to get. I knew the Dutch had a reputation as shrewd traders and merchants. Looking at my countrymen, tiring of the back and forth, I was ready to disavow my heritage. "What would be my father's debt in gold?"

Abraham reached for a piece of parchment and quill. He started jotting down figures. With a flourish he pushed the paper toward me. "One hundred pounds."

The amount was staggering, and likely an inflated number. He must have seen my shock.

"Bad decisions and interest. I can fully document the debt."

At that point I was almost glad our ship had never reached port here. Considering my options, I sat and watched as they grew even more uncomfortable. "I can pay you ten percent as a surety. That's all we have."

They looked at each other, considering the offer. "Very well. That will show good faith. Now for the split."

"I'll take no less than an eighty percent share."

"After your debt and expenses are paid."

"Done." Handing over ten pounds of gold would make a significant dent in our reserves, but I was looking forward, thinking it would be about the amount it would cost to fully provision the ship. Once our holds were full we could make our own decisions.

"Very well. Abraham will draw up the contract. Your ship will be allowed to anchor here and provision."

For all the talk, it had turned out in our favor, but I was intrigued about my father. "Do you have the communication with my father?"

"We have his proposal. There is enough detail, I believe, to give you a place to start."

My father had faded from my memory over the years. The chance to reconnect with him, even if it was through a ream of paper, excited me. "I'd like to have a look."

"We'll have to insist on the gold first."

"Once my ship is here." They looked relieved the negotiations had been completed and rose.

"Abraham will show you the town and introduce you to the merchants that might be of help in provisioning your ship."

One at a time they filed out of the room, leaving me with Abraham. "I could use some air."

He nodded and led me out of the room, down the hall, and out of the building. On arrival, I had been taken directly here and had seen nothing of the town. Now, as we walked the main street, I noticed the different-colored buildings. Abraham had started the tour with an explanation that some governor along the line had decreed that no building would be painted white. The result was a palette of colors. The town was neat and organized, much as you would expect from the Dutch.

As Abraham guided me from one shop to another, I kept an eye on the harbor, anticipating the arrival of the *Dorado*. Trying to calculate the time to determine when to expect them, I realized even in the best of circumstances they were still several hours away.

It was then that I realized the Dutch might have been craftier than I had anticipated. With a letter promising cooperation written in my own hand, the crew would not likely have resisted a boarding party. As it was our own skiff returning with the letter, they would be unprepared if there was foul play involved.

The thought made me anxious. I tried to dismiss the feeling, reminding myself that this negotiation was not personal, but business with the Dutch West India Company. If there was a glimmer of hope that the venture would be profitable, they would do whatever was required. Even the prospect of recouping some of my father's debt would be enough to keep them honest.

Chapter 41

The Dutch had a reputation for being shrewd, and they proved true to their word. With the *Dorado* anchored in the harbor, Mason supervised provisioning the ship, while Rhames drilled the men and serviced the weaponry. Within a week of arrival we were in as good a shape as we had been for the last two years.

Henrik had taken the ten bars of gold as surety. My father's debt aside, that would put the town's merchants in the black, for our bills to date. I learned a little more about my countrymen as the week went by, and quite a bit about my father. A series of letters were handed over to me. The first, dated, two years before we set sail for America, was his initial query. Over the next two years the correspondence piled up and finally ended with a contract.

After reading the letters, it was like my own voice springing from the pages; I had little doubt my father was the writer. The excitement was palpable, though after careful study—unless there was more evidence—the facts seemed questionable.

The West India Company had approved his contract, loaning the stated ten-thousand guilders as an advance against earnings. As I calculated how much the trip and other expenses would have been, it dawned on me, as a cruel irony, that Gasparilla had taken the lion's share. Resigning myself to the facts, I started to dig into the research. Though not as fanatical as the Spanish at documenting everything, the Dutch were well organized and, with the help of an aging librarian, I soon had in front of me several large books and maps.

Shayla was by my side as we waded through the information. With the exception of a short period ending with the Napoleonic wars in 1815, when the islands were under French rule, the Dutch had administered the islands since the 1600s. The long period of stability had left an uninterrupted historical account of the area. Though Dutch was the official language, Spanish was commonplace. Fortunately, the language hadn't changed much over the centuries, and I was still able to read most of the Dutch accounts while Shayla worked on the Spanish.

Piracy and slavery had both played prominent roles in Curacao's history, but there was no longer evidence of either. In fact, the region, largely unsuitable for planting due to its arid climate, with the decline of the slave trade seemed to have fallen on hard times. Slowly, we were able to separate the relevant journals from the other record books, and our history lesson started.

Brazil had been under Dutch rule in 1628 when Henriques had found refuge there. His retirement didn't last long, as the Portuguese took control of the country in 1630. The Inquisitors weren't far behind and Henriques had started north, hoping to settle in the Dutch-ruled Netherland Antilles. An infamous and wealthy pirate in what was then a pirate's den was no place for Henriques and he moved on, but not before losing his flagship off a nearby island. It was that ship my father had sought.

Shayla pushed a journal toward me. "There's an account in Spanish here."

I'd come a long way in learning Spanish, but the two-hundred-year-old writing was like a different language. My eyes drifted away from the text and focused on a hand-drawn map on the adjacent page.

"What island is that?" I pointed to an oval-shaped island with another, smaller island just off a north-facing bay.

"Bonaire. Just to the east of us," Shayla said.

Three main islands comprised the Netherland Antilles: Aruba, Bonaire, and Curacao. From what I had seen of Curacao, it was covered with quite a bit of lava, remnants of long-dead volcanoes. The presence of volcanic rock and limestone meant there would be caves. A sudden storm had swept us into a cenote, a limestone cavern system in Cozumel. After a wild ride through the underground river we had found Herniques's cache in a cavern near its end. The coincidence in this island's geologic composition needed serious consideration.

"Maybe something to have a look at. From the map here, the eastern exposure looks promising." The location added to the authenticity of my father's claim. If Henriques was in trouble he would have secreted his treasure, and where better than a cave accessible only from the sea? The prevailing winds made the location difficult to access, but if the treasure had been hidden there, it would also be hard to find. We knew Henriques had survived to place the cache in Cozumel, but my gut told me my father was onto something.

"We should tell the others," Shayla said, rubbing her eyes.

I was tired of sifting through documents in the dim light of the library. Tucking the journal under my arm, I squinted in the bright sunlight as we left the building. The pier was still busy with small boats shuttling goods to the ship. We hopped on the next boat headed for the *Dorado*, to the dismay of the man at the helm, for our weight meant he could carry less cargo. Reaching the rope ladder, I couldn't help but smile as I watched Shayla climb ahead of me. Now that I knew she was pregnant, I could see her curves had shifted slightly. My heart nearly skipped a beat when her foot slipped, but she easily regained her balance and swung onto the deck. The incident served to remind me that we needed to find a safe port for her to have the baby.

The crew was all smiles as they watched the provisions come aboard. Never in our travels had we had this much in our stores. Pigs and chickens were dropped into the aft hold, promising a welcome respite from our diet that had previously consisted mainly of fish.

"How much more?" I asked Mason.

"Should about do it. We'll do a walk-through later. How about a destination?"

"Bonaire."

"There's nothing but bones and flamingos on that spit of land."

"And treasure."

His expression told me he was skeptical. Leading him to the binnacle, I took the book from my bag and laid out the marked page on the chart table.

"By God, if it's not the same bastard."

"Henriques," I confirmed.

"And you're thinking he uses a cave once and he'll have done it again?"

"Makes sense. There is an account of his flagship being wrecked here. That's a bad spot to face a blow or a battle."

"Aye. Prevailing winds make it a lee shore. You say there's caves there?"

I tapped the Spanish writing as if I could read it. Mason couldn't either, but we stared at the writing like it spoke to us. "It's only a day's sail. No harm in having a look."

"Right, these bastards seem a bit more hospitable than Lafitte or the Spanish."

"Just don't cross them where business is concerned. They'd sell their first-born for a profit."

"Your countrymen … " He left the rest unsaid.

"Right, then. On the tide tomorrow."

I walked away to seek out Rhames. As usual he was in front of the armory. With a cutlass braced between his foot and opposite leg, he rubbed a stone against the blade. A pile of sharpened steel glistened in the sun beside him. For now, he was doing what he'd always done; it would be at a time that steel was needed that we would see how his injury affected him.

"We've got a treasure to find," I said, picking up one of the daggers in the pile and running my hand down its razor-sharp edge.

"Lot of good it'll do me."

Though his demeanor betrayed nothing, the tone of his voice did. The world was changing for both of us; me with a family on the way, and Rhames with his injury. I'd been doing a good deal of thinking on the matter.

"You were the one that told me about the bold pirates never getting old," I said to him.

He exhaled. "There's old pirates and bold pirates. Ain't many old, bold ones." He looked around the deck to see if anyone was within earshot, then lowered his voice. "Aye, but it'd be nice to choose the time of your undoing."

I sat next to him and picked up a stone and dagger. Though not as adept as he was, the feel of steel against stone felt good. "With the baby coming, I'm in the same position."

"You're still a lad. Your better years lay ahead. I'm an old pirate …" He tried to leave the last bit unsaid.

"A legend, more like it. Take a step forward. Pick your battles and train your men. A good general doesn't have to be in the thick of it."

He gave me one of his queer looks that told me he didn't understand. My father, and then Gasparilla, had ensured I had an education. I knew of the great generals: Alexander, Caesar, and more. "I've got your back."

"And I appreciate that, but maybe it's time for me to cash out and find a woman who can tolerate me."

"If we find this treasure, we may all be able to cash out."

Chapter 42

STEVEN BECKER

Gasparilla had preached that knowing your enemy was crucial to victory. The advice had served him well until the end. Knowing he was a target of the U.S. Navy, he had decided to call it quits. The morning of the fateful day, he had assembled the crew on the beach of Gasparilla Island to split our hoarded treasure, after which we would go our separate ways. Though the old pirate knew his enemy well enough to know it was time to retire, the Navy had studied their enemy as well. Disguising one of their frigates as a merchantman, they had sailed it close enough to our gathering to draw our attention.

Gasparilla had taken the bait and sailed the *Floridablanca* to her demise. Along with nine other crew assigned to guard the treasure, I had watched as the USS Constitution sank our ship. Gasparilla, wrapping himself in the anchor chain, had plunged to his death. That day was the beginning of a new life. My mentor might have died that day, but his lessons lived on inside me.

We had been lied to, stolen from, and almost blown up by our enemies. Now I had to decide what to do about the Dutch. They were a conundrum, and I wasn't sure if I could trust them. Finally, it came down to business—and that was what they were all about.

"We've got full holds and a contract." I held up the paper like it meant something.

"You'd trust the bastards over a piece of paper?" Rhames snorted.

The document had been passed around the group, but aside from Shayla, Mason, and myself, I wasn't sure if the others could read.

"We've been all over this cursed sea and you expect this piece of paper to mean something?" Mason asked.

I understood their skepticism. The last few nights had been sleepless, as we wondered about the same things. In the end, it was Dutch history and not my heritage that swayed me. The Dutch East and West India Companies had ruled through trade, only resorting to violence to enforce their contracts.

"We've got nothing to lose by having a look, have we? If there's nothing there, we've paid for our provisions, we'll just move on."

With some reluctance heads started to nod.

"Ain't no point sitting here, then. Little to do in this blasted town anyway," Rhames said.

"Right, then. We sail with the tide. I'll be checking the gear, then." I walked away, ending the conversation. Mason and I had already plotted our course. He would have command until we reached our destination. The divers followed me to the forward hold, where we had stored our equipment. Fresh lard was applied to the hoses and the pumps were checked. With two sets of headgear and the pumps from our old ship, we were well-equipped if we found a likely place. After a thorough inspection I left the divers to store the gear.

Just as I walked away from the divers, I heard Mason call for sail to be raised and the anchor weighed. Swearing that what happened on our departure from Grand Cayman would not happen again, I climbed the mast for a view of the surrounding water. The harbor lay quiet and, with no sails on the horizon, I relaxed in my perch as we got underway.

The last week had brought to the surface things that I had buried deep within me. Between the research, contracts, and provisioning of the ship, I'd had little time to ponder my past. As the ship settled into the seas I found myself thinking about my father. At first it had been a shock, and I couldn't deny my disappointment on finding out he'd left me saddled with a debt. On reflection, though, my opinion changed. It was exactly as I would have done had I been in his place, and I found myself admiring him. Finding the treasure he'd sought would be sweet justice and a good starting point for our new life.

We sailed east. Close-hauled and just a few points from the wind, the ship felt different than the older brigantines we were accustomed to. With only two square-sails, the schooner was considerably more maneuverable. The masts rose higher above the deck and, taking the seas almost head-on, I was not as comfortable as on the slower, downwind ships. As I was getting my sea legs I saw a figure climbing toward me. Seeing it was Shayla, my heart leapt into my throat. Cresting a wave, we dropped into the trough and I watched her grab for an adjacent line for additional support. At least she was being careful and soon was beside me

"She's like an unbroken stallion," she said with a smile that betrayed no fear.

"Takes a bit of time to get used to." I knew better than to ask or order her down, though she seemed steadier than I felt at such a height.

"Thinking about your pa?" she asked, as she settled into the rhythm of the ship.

"I never would have thought."

"Don't let it cloud your judgment."

"Just have a look, then we're off to the Horn."

"And a good day that'll be."

We stood together in silence, both wondering what fate held for us. Some believed you couldn't control your destiny, but I had a dream and was determined to see it through.

As the crow flew it was only thirty miles between the islands, and as the sun was setting Bonaire appeared before us. The area I aimed to investigate was on the other side of the island, adding another ten miles, but the chart showed deep water, and if the wind remained favorable we would risk the detour at night. If nothing else, our experience had shown us that when treasure was involved it was best to act decisively. Leaving Shayla to keep watch, I climbed down to speak to Mason.

"Deep water all around."

"I'm with you. The sooner we get this business over with the better." He surveyed the water as if waiting for a ship to appear. Leaving him to his demons, I went forward to check on the divers. The gear was stowed and ready for tomorrow. It was up to me to find a use for it.

With the wind coming out of the southeast, we dropped the hook in a sheltered inlet just shy of the northern point of the island. With only a handful of miles between us and our goal, I went below to try and get some rest. For once I was glad that Shayla had remained on watch and dropped to the bunk, where I immediately fell asleep.

For the first time in weeks, I slept through the night. Hoping it was a harbinger of things to come, I rose with the sun and went on deck. The bell had yet to ring signaling the morning watch, and the ship remained quiet with only three men on duty. I relieved all but the man in the rigging and went to the binnacle, where I pulled out Mason's chart and studied the island. There was little detail plotted, other than a small island near an adjacent bay.

Trying to visualize the island from Henriques's perspective,

I ran my finger along the line marking the shore hoping it would somehow magically stop where the treasure was located. Before my divination worked I was interrupted by Mason.

"If I were wanting to stash my loot, I'd think about here." His thick finger landed on a small inlet just around the point.

Small marks showed a rocky shore, just the kind of formation where caves were located. "It's on the weather side, though."

"You'd be trying to hide something, you wouldn't make it easy."

He was right about that. We'd found the treasure in Cozumel by a stroke of luck. A storm had dumped us into a cenote, one of the island's underground cave systems, and the sudden flood had taken us right to it. I hadn't thought about it, but Henriques placed it coming from the sea, not from land as we had found it. Dawn lit the rocky shore and I studied the island, trying to think like Henriques.

"Right, then. Let's have a look." I moved my gaze out to sea, where a ship could come on us from any direction. "This whole area's too exposed for my liking."

"You're right about that. The minute we drop the skiffs, we're sitting ducks."

I knew him to be a worrier and tried to waive my own fears. Moving to the mast, I yanked the cord on the bell. Heads popped up from where they had slept and the deck was soon awash in activity. Mason had the anchor hauled and we were underway. There was no need for full sail as our destination was only a few miles away, and by the time we reached the inlet we were ready to drop the skiff and see if my father was right.

Chapter 43

Under any other conditions the entry to the cave would have been invisible. With a light breeze the seas were near flat, and still the opening was only a dark sliver against the water. We'd passed it by twice before returning for a closer look. The coast was comprised of porous rock formed into cliffs from a long-past volcano. Though a different material from the limestone caverns in the Yucatan, the characteristics were much the same.

The ebb tide gave us a better view into the dark cavern, but with the current streaming through it we would have to wait several hours to enter, or risk being swept out to sea. Setting a light anchor, I decided to take the opportunity to explore the area hoping to find an alternate, and safer, entry point. One of the divers and I swam the twenty feet to shore and climbed the rocky cliff. Rising less than ten feet from the water, the cliffs were easily scaled and we found ourselves on a flat plain.

Scratching a stick into the thin layer of topsoil, I found the same material that lay exposed on the cliffs. As the sun beat down on us, we moved around the area looking for any anomalies that might help our search. We explored for a solid hour, finding nothing but dry soil, cactuses, and iguanas, none of which were any use to us. As we climbed back down the deep-blue water beckoned. The gentle mist created by the waves breaking against the rocks was refreshing, and looking down at the cave entrance I could barely see the water moving.

The slack tide would allow us several hours to explore the cave. The skiff arrived to pick us up, and the diver and I remained in the water. Hanging onto the side of the small boat, the men above placed the helmets over our heads and adjusted the hoses. Not thinking that we would need to descend I wasn't sure if the gear was even necessary, but I didn't want to be caught unprepared. Once air flowed through the hoses, we gave the signal to each other and the crew above, then dropped under the surface.

Immediately the shadows from the entrance turned the water around us near-black. Hoping there would be some light, perhaps from a lava tube, once we entered the cave, I felt around the perimeter of the entrance and, finding plenty of depth below us, descended and swam into the opening. Darkness enveloped us as the dim light from the entrance faded to black. Using my hands I tried to navigate the cavern, but without light the search was in vain. We had failed to anticipate the conditions and were not equipped to explore any further. The delay would cost us a day, but we now knew when the tide would be slack again.

Reaching out to find the diver, who just a second ago had been next to me, my hand grasped nothing but water and I flung my arms around hoping to locate him. Disoriented, it took a long second to acclimate myself and, finding the dim light emanating from the entrance, I focused on that and breathed the stale air supplied by the pumps. A tug on my helmet brought me back to reality and I realized that as long as we retained our gear, there was no chance of becoming lost. The hoses were our life-line for both air and the outside world.

The realization settled me down and I started back into the cave, this time swinging my arms in an attempt to find the other diver's hoses. Once I found them they would lead me to him. Swimming with the cumbersome gear was near impossible and I settled into a dog paddle. My knee struck something hard and I found myself able to stand. Fortunately, the helmet protected my head when I slammed it on the ceiling of the cave, but still I saw stars from the impact into the hard rock.

The cave appeared to be at an end, but I could still feel water flowing past me. Carefully I continued using my hands to feel in front of me. While we might be able to light the first section by floating lanterns inside, as I eased myself sideways and down through a narrow opening that was fully submerged I realized that whatever lay ahead we would not be able to illuminate.

All thoughts of the other diver were gone as I proceeded. If he had ventured this deep into the system I surely would have found his hoses by now. Assuming that he had fled the claustrophobic cave, I continued. After passing through the narrow channel, I could see light ahead and was able to stand. This time I rose slowly out of the water and soon felt the weight of the headgear.

As I stepped out of the pool I could feel the temperature difference between the water and the air, the cause of the condensation. It was risky for me to remove the helmet. Once it was off I might not be able to replace it myself, but thinking back on the path I had taken to reach this point, there was only the one narrow section that was fully filled with water where I would have to hold my breath to swim through on the return. Kneeling down in the shallow water, I lay on my back and eased the helmet from my head.

I wasn't sure what to expect when I took my first breath, but the air was clean if hot and stuffy. I blinked, realizing it was sweat in my eyes and not just water. Thinking I might have stumbled on a portal to the underworld instead of a treasure cache, I blinked again and tried to find the source of the light. Slowly my eyes acclimated and I saw there wasn't a single source, but many small flickers from the ceiling. I was soon able to see the sunlight penetrating the porous rock above me that evenly lit the entire cave.

Leaving the headgear at the edge of the water I proceeded onto a beach that was more rock than sand, it looked like one of several of the black-sand beaches we had seen in our travels. Leaning over to inspect the material I saw what appeared to be a boot print. Unarmed and unprepared, my first thought was that I wasn't alone. Standing in the middle of the cavern I was exposed and defenseless. There was nothing I could do about it except retreat back into the water. Taking several steps, I studied the small sections of sand interspersed between the rocks and saw several more prints.

Standing frozen and exposed, calf-deep in the water, I waited. After a few minutes the only sounds I heard were the wind whistling through the same openings that filtered the light and the gentle lapping of the water on the beach. But my field of vision ended short of the cave walls, where there could still be danger lurking in their darkness. Though I can't explain it, I've felt the presence of unseen men before. The thing was, I didn't feel anything like that now.

Moving out of the water I turned to the right and, being careful not to disturb any of the prints in the sand, proceeded with my inspection. Finding the sidewall of the cave, I used its rough surface to guide me as I moved to the left. After completing almost a full circle I found myself back where I had started—with no sign of treasure or man other than the foot-prints in the sand.

Discouraged, I sat on one of the larger rocks. Thinking about what I was missing, I saw the headgear I had set on the beach jerk back. I jumped up and ran toward it, but it pulled back again, this time submerging. Entering the water, I reached for it—finding not the helmet, but Blue. I must have been gone longer than expected, or the other diver had returned thinking I was missing.

Blue climbed out of the water and looked around. "Someone has been here." He leaned over one of the prints in the sand.

"It appears so, but I can't make any sense out of it."

He continued to study the footprint, then moved on to the next. Watching him work, I couldn't help but admire his skill in seeing what I could not. Instead of heading for the back of the cave as I had done, he continued following what appeared to be a man's tracks.

"Big man. Expensive boots," was all he said as he followed the tracks of what he assumed was the leader of the party that had preceded us.

I knew better than to interrupt him and followed behind, giving him plenty of room to work. Several times he clucked his tongue and backtracked. Thinking he was going to fare no better than I, he suddenly stopped near the back corner of the cave and stood on one of the larger rocks.

I saw it then, a cluster of footprints surrounding the rock. But it wasn't a single rock at all.

Chapter 44

Were it not for the footprints, I would have passed right by that section of wall. Blue had found it and I let him remove the first stone. Placed as skillfully as a master mason might have done, what appeared to be a solid rock-wall came apart one stone at a time. At first I was worried about destroying the footprints, but the excitement of the find overrode any desire to preserve history.

The wall was soon at waist level and we peered inside to see an extension of the cave. It was a small area, but looked to be empty. I wasn't discouraged, though, after seeing how well whoever constructed the stone wall had done their job. I suspected more of the same inside. Together, Blue and I removed the last of the stones and stepped inside the alcove. The same phenomenon that allowed light to filter into the rest of the cave permeated here as well.

Blue had his nose to the ground like a bloodhound while I ran my hands over the rough rock of the walls. Inspecting every crack like it might have held the secret, I worked my way around, but found nothing. Leaning against the wall I watched

Blue, who appeared to have narrowed his search down to one area.

"There are no prints here," he said, rubbing his hands over the sand and rock of the cave's floor.

"What do you make of it?"

"These marks. They were made with a tool." He lay flat on the ground, placing his eye level with the surface.

I squatted to get a better look, but failed to see whatever he saw. "Do you think they buried something here?"

"There's no other explanation. Why go through all the work of building the wall and then bury it?"

His question didn't need an answer. If someone went to all this trouble, we had found what my father was looking for and it was likely substantial. "We'll need more men and shovels."

"There could be traps." Blue continued to study the ground.

"Right, then. Only one way to find out. We won't find it with just the two of us digging with our hands." He nodded and rose. We could barely contain our excitement as we retraced our steps back to the pool of water. The headgear lay just outside of the water and I decided to leave it as a lifeline. Taking the bucket that was the helmet, I dragged the lines clear of the water and looped them several times around a boulder-sized rock. A tug on the hoses wedged the bucket into a gap in the rocks.

With one hand each looped on the hoses we made our way back to the narrow passage. After taking several deep breaths I dove down, careful not to release my grip, and started pulling myself through. Reaching the other side, I breathed deeply and waited for Blue. His head appeared seconds later and we continued to follow the hoses. Either the tide had come in faster than I anticipated or we had been gone longer than I had figured. Either way the entrance was now below water. Treading water above the spot where the hoses exited the cave, we heard the waves crashing against the rock just outside the opening.

Swimming through the mouth of the cave was not a problem; it was when we surfaced outside that the waves could grab us and slam us back toward the sharp rocks. There was no other way, except to wait for the tide to change, and by that time it would be dark.

"Swim hard until you're well clear," I cautioned Blue as I inhaled. My chest was full and I dropped under. Keeping one hand on the hoses and the other ready to pull myself past the wall, I started to exit the cave. Light guided my progress and the white froth on the water above told me I had cleared the opening. But I knew better than to relax as a surge took me and, without my hold on the hoses, would have flung me against the cliff. With both hands now pulling me forward I was able to make some progress. Knowing the surge would end with a lull that released the water back to the sea, I waited and when I felt the surface tension change reached hand over hand, grabbing hose as I pulled myself clear of the wash. Blue was right behind me and we surfaced together.

The look on our faces must have said it all, but it was premature relief when I saw how close the skiff was to the cliff.

"Row us out past the soup," I called to the men manning the oar.

We were soon pulled past the dangerous breakers and into the swell. The men pulled us aboard and we told them about the cave. When they heard that we hadn't found anything I felt their spirits drop, but I assured them that what we had found was important, though it would have to wait for the morning.

———

AFTER RETURNING to the ship I could feel the excitement in the air after Blue and I told Shayla, Lucy, and the rest of the crew. Mason was still opposed to putting the ship at risk by bringing it around the point, and we were forced to draw straws to see who would man the skiffs. Everyone was in a jubilant mood except for Rhames, who sat brooding off to the side. With our plan set, we settled in for what, at least for me, would be a sleepless night.

The morning broke clear and calm, I hoped a sign of what was to come. Blue and I had been able to locate the opening from inside by the hoses running through it. As we sat waiting, it was impossible to see the cavern until the tide dropped enough to reveal the top of the opening.

Blue and I were to go back, along with several divers with shovels and picks. I had embellished on the difficulty of the narrow passage to discourage the less-experienced from wanting to join us. As he hauled a rope in with him, we followed Blue into the darkness. After securing the line to a boulder, we moved immediately to the alcove.

"Where do you think?" I asked Blue.

The freedmen stood with skeptical looks on their faces. Like me, they had no idea what Blue saw, either. He marked a large X on the ground with his heel and stood back while the men started to dig. It was easy work and a hole about six-feet across and two-feet deep was quickly excavated. Taking a break, the men's skeptical looks returned.

While they rested, Blue took a pick and attacked the center of the hole. I rose to join him and we soon had another foot of sand and rock removed, but still there was no sign of any treasure. At this point I was starting to wonder, but Blue continued slamming the pointed end of the pick into the dirt until finally we heard a thunk, the sound of metal on wood instead of rock echoing through the alcove. The men jumped up and pushed us away, taking to the task with new life.

Blue never told me why he'd chosen that spot to dig, but a large void opened below the excavation. Inside it were a dozen chests that each took two strong men to lift. The wary expressions on the faces of the men around me told the story. We had been deceived before, any celebration would wait. An hour later the hole was empty and we were faced with the task of moving the heavy chests. The search and digging had consumed our window of opportunity for the day, forcing us to leave the chests in the alcove in order to escape the cave before the tide prevented it.

Back on the ship, our excitement turned to nervous tension, as we knew the treasure sat unprotected. I could see each man eyeing his neighbor and counting heads to make sure no one disappeared. After a long night, dawn broke and we set out to retrieve our find.

Shayla and I had a reserved moment together, but we both knew this wasn't over until the treasure was secured, and we had moved on to other waters. After what we'd been through, what they held was anyone's guess, but at least we would be rich again.

The night had given me time to think. Worried about the weight of the chests, I decided to unload them and shuttle the treasure out of the cave with a series of burlap sacks tied to a line. There was a chance that one might snag on a rock and break, but I couldn't see getting the chests out intact. How Henriques' men had gotten them in would remain a mystery.

The same men as the day before were tasked with the job of extracting the treasure, and we quickly swam through the chambers, relieved to find the chests sitting as we left them.

Chapter 45

The day's recovery had gone well, my plan working to perfection, but hampered by the rising tide we only had time to recover half the treasure. Leaving half the cache, even if it was just for the night, was unsettling, especially since we had been in this situation before. All we could do was stare anxiously across the water and think about the wealth we had previously left in our wake. This effort proved different and the following day we recovered the rest. It had been a taxing few days and I went to bed as soon as our newly found riches were stashed in the bilge.

With twice as much treasure as was found in Henriques's cache in Cozumel, we were all wealthy—again. Now, time was our enemy. Staying another night offshore of Bonaire was the last thing any of us wanted to do. With only the skinny rock protecting our flank, the approaches were wide open. With our newfound wealth aboard, and after having been betrayed several times before, we were worried

That night, without my knowledge Rhames broke out the good rum and shared it with the crew. As you would expect, at first it was a raucous celebration, but with the alcohol flowing it soon turned into a one-sided debate about screwing the Dutch.

It was near midnight when the sound of drunken voices woke me. Quickly I dressed and headed for the deck.

"Right, then. What's this nonsense about?"

"Why should we give the bastards a share? It was your own father that found it." Rhames wobbled as he spoke.

The crew cheered behind him. If I didn't do something quickly the gathering would likely turn into a pirate meeting and no good would come of that. An argument at this point would solve nothing—what I needed was time. Time for the night to end, time for the effects of the alcohol to wear off, and time for sober men to be reasoned with. Glancing seaward, I would have preferred to see a sail on the horizon than to deal with the rabble standing in front of me.

Shayla came to my rescue. Exiting the companionway, she stood beside me and raised her hands for quiet, waiting calmly. I saw Phillip shyly poke his head from the opening and wondered what she was up to.

"What are you doing?" I whispered.

"They want a party, let's give them a reason."

"Now?"

"Why not?"

"And you're sure?"

"If we don't do something they'll burn down the ship."

She didn't wait for my answer. "Gather round, everyone." She waited until the group formed in front of us. "You all know we are having a baby, and I can't think of a better time to marry."

A cheer went up; the Dutch had been forgotten.

"Who's going to conduct the ceremony?" I asked.

"My father's done it before." She called for Phillip, who came to stand between us.

Under the star-speckled sky, with more wealth on board

than we could spend in several lifetimes, we were married. Unfortunately, as we were the only sober ones aboard, we took watch directly after the ceremony. The exhausted and inebriated men soon collapsed on deck. Aside from the snoring men, the only sound we could hear was the water lapping against the ship.

The next morning we set sail for Curacao. There was no heated debate, merely a short conversation where the crew agreed to honor the contract with the Dutch. We had burnt enough bridges behind us; it was time to start building them instead. Our arrival in Willemstad was a sober affair. Surprised at both our honesty and the riches we had found, we were treated well and, after provisioning, weighed anchor for the uncharted waters ahead.

Over the next few days we crossed the equator and, just after leaving Trinidad to port, entered the Atlantic. With the Caribbean in our wake, the adversity that had dampened our previous endeavors was broken, and we could only hope our luck would change.

About the Author

Always looking for a new location or adventure to write about, Steven Becker can usually be found on or near the water. He splits his time between Tampa and the Florida Keys - paddling, sailing, diving, fishing or exploring.

Find out more by visiting www.stevenbeckerauthor.com or contact me directly at booksbybecker@gmail.com.

Get my starter library First Bite for Free!
when you sign up for my newsletter

http://eepurl.com/-obDj

First Bite contains the first book in each of Steven Becker's series:

- **Wood's Reef**
- **Pirate**
- **Bonefish Blues**

By joining you will receive one or two emails a month about what I'm doing and special offers.

Your contact information and privacy are important to me. I will not spam or share your email with anyone.

Wood's Reef

"A riveting tale of intrigue and terrorism, Key West characters in their full glory! Fast paced and continually changing direction Mr Becker has me hooked on his skillful and adventurous tales from the Conch Republic!"

Pirate

"A gripping tale of pirate adventure off the coast of 19th Century Florida!"

Bonefish Blues *"I just couldn't put this book down. A great plot filled with action. Steven Becker brings each character to life, allowing the reader to become immersed in the plot."*

Get them now (http://eepurl.com/-obDj)

Made in the USA
Monee, IL
27 March 2021

63994635R00152